SUDDEN TRAVELLER

SUDDEN TRAVELLER

– *Stories* –

SARAH HALL

FABER & FABER

First published in 2019
by Faber & Faber Limited
74–77 Great Russell Street
London WC1B 3DA

Typeset by Typo•glyphix, Burton-on-Trent, DE14 3HE
Printed and bound in England by CPI Group (UK) Ltd,
Croydon, CRO 4YY

A CIP record for this book is available from the British Library

ISBN 978-0-571-34504-5

2 4 6 8 10 9 7 5 3 1

H'e

But somehow, somewhere, sometime soon
Upon this wild abandoned star

from 'Spell', Nick Cave

Contents

ix

M

A warm, damp, starless night in the city. The last night of summer. Darkness moves like an ocean above the roofs and streetlights. The wind is directionless, confusing the trees, loosening sidings and tiles. Creatures of flight have put themselves away, under the eaves, down chimneys; raptors are tucked behind bevelled glass spires. The windows of houses stand open, venting air, exhaust and the fume of falling leaves. The lungs of sleepers are evolving. It is the hour between prayers.

She wakes. As she turns in bed, away from the body on the other side, she notices a pain. It's low down, on the right-hand side, a soreness like appendicitis. But she has no appendix, only a surgical cleft in the skin, left over from childhood. The organ was removed after rupture and septicaemia; her body flooded with poison, the school nurse having told her twice to go back to class, the ambulance moving sluggishly down the valley's roads. Lucky to be alive, the surgeon said, once her blood had clarified. Her father bought a new car while she was recovering, the first soft-top in the village, and he drove it into the hospital grounds, sounding the horn outside her window. Who can that be, her mother asked. She was driven home triumphantly, lilting to the side, exhilarated, the wind racing through her hair.

So began a life's contract of survival and compensation. The metal breath of the tractor as it rolled, inches from her, down the steep upper field, its brake having failed, crushing her father under its huge rear wheel. The estate's payout for the loss of its manager, enough to fund law school and a basement flat in London. The motorcycle accident when she was nineteen, riding pillion with a boyfriend who'd told her that he loved her, who visited the spinal unit once, saw the halo screwed to her scalp to immobilise her neck, and didn't come again. Six months later she saw him in a bar, or rather he saw her, un-killed, risen, beautiful, faint red holes along her brow. The ankle broken from falling in Appalachia: airlifted down off the trail after three days, unconscious, dehydrated, bone exposed through the skin, clean as an arrowhead, the rescue message with her GPS coordinates delayed by weather. Every glass of water after, a minor ecstasy. Events to chart pain's signature. Reaction to malaria prophylactic, transit of a kidney stone, wisdom tooth extraction. The night she was forced, while her mother was away in hospital. The morning she was forced again. She has always left room for worse, the unimaginable, and what may follow.

Comparatively, this is not severe. But it is unlike anything before. She sits up, holds her stomach. What? Not cramps; her periods are insignificant, her body having shed its viable eggs the decade before. Not a virus, though it's the weakest hour of immunity, the time sickness usually comes. She lies back down, tries not to wake Ilias, and waits for it to pass. It is the most peculiar sensation. A hot zipping feeling under the skin, moving from hip to belly. No, *unzipping.*

Her lover stirs, but continues to sleep. Tick, tick, tick, across the abdomen, as if sutures are being unstrung. She tenses, resists, but then allows it, expects it, as one might surrender to contractions. Heat radiates up her torso, and beads of sweat begin to trickle underneath her breasts. The sheets dampen. After an hour, the discomfort fades. She gets up, opens the window wider, drifts back to sleep inside a turbine of cool air.

In the morning, nothing remains, though she feels a little clumsy, knocks her water glass on the bedside table and soaks a book. She gets up to shut the window, collects the yellow leaves blown in. Ilias is awake, propped on an arm, watching. Her legs are stiff, uncooperative as she bends. She does not feel usual. Nevertheless, they make love, on their sides, facing each other, an angle of great pleasure and intimacy. Memories of the night interfere. She struggles. After a few minutes he realises, moves on top, comes on her belly and apologises. Say you're not sorry, she says, and smiles. I'm not sorry. But your sheets? No, it was me, she says. I think I over-heated. He kisses her. Re-enters. Wetter. These are acceptable risks; from the start, they have not been care-ful. The blood is loaded in the right place; her nerves are ready. This time, release. She cries into his shoulder, leaves a mark.

She lets him make the coffee in her kitchen, black, bitter. They dress, talk for a few minutes, but there is no time. She takes the stairs down with him. As he leaves, he turns and waves, looks up. He loves the building, its sculpted brutalist concrete, the distinctive middle tower. He is young, works for an architect, low in the chain, but is gifted, she suspects. The firm is responsible for the fast-altering skyline, the smoked-glass high-rises at the sea end of the river, which mirror the marsh they are deposing. Twice a week, more often lately, they meet in a bar for a drink, spend the night. It's enough.

The street is littered with bright leaves, pulp and small branches. There's a cider aroma, and the smell of latrines, flushed gutters, sodden fur. She walks to her office, remembering other autumns, their lucidity, bronze northern light. When she arrives, her secretary looks agitated, hands her a message, a request that would not usually be filtered through, and a prepared file. I know this place, the secretary tells her, it's called the

M

Haven. My sister and I lived there for six months. Please look. She takes the held-out file. Thank you, Katya.

The next night, the pain returns, around the same time, folding her double. She is alone, and it is worse. The bands of muscles seem to be spasming, pulling her midriff tight, pulling it apart. She could almost put her fingers in. And a definite fever, fugue-like, tubercular, the sheet sticking to her back. Not nausea but a desire to retch, as if her tongue is curling down her throat. Is it the flu? Has she picked up an infection? What other organ has gone wrong? She shifts position, gradually, inch by inch, one side, then the other, but she cannot find relief. In the morning she will call the doctor. She tries to think. Of the date of her last period, date of her last screenings, the year her mother died. Of relevant stories, misaligned pregnancies, tumours, anomalies. She tries to think.

When dawn arrives the riven feeling is again passing, and the delirium. She falls asleep, misses the alarm. She is woken by the annunciation of bright mid-morning. It is a busy day, a partners' meeting, lunch with an old friend who has moved back after divorce. In the afternoon she visits the Haven, which has been bought – it is unclear by whom – and is under threat of closure. At the shelter are women who have been abused, tormented, even shot. The children play families with each other, swap stories like war trophies, are careful with their names. A girl with pale-green eyes, a teenager, holds a toy dog to her chest, an item much too young for her. Black and white, like a Border sheepdog. She will not put it down. The staff are tired, and overworked, and also scarred. She accepts the case, her first pro bono work in years. Back at the office her secretary hugs her, awkwardly, and thanks her. The day ends. The absence of pain is a place of forgetting, a country far away. She does not call the doctor.

That evening, she meets Ilias again. A new bar, above a sex shop. The walls are sombre navy, the woodwork charcoal, fashionably, darkly Victorian. Ineffectual candles pulse in the gloom. The drinks are exquisite, herbal spirits, very strong, mixed by muscled barwomen in leather aprons. They flirt, enjoy each other, as they always do. But a certainty is forming in her mind. It will – it must – stop soon. He holds her hand across the table, uninhibited. For the first time in a long while she feels emotion heeling in her. He has such kindness, openness. He seems full of blue light, in the blue room. The men around him in the dim corners flicker, faces razored like ringmasters, eyes full of coils. She can almost taste their lust, like brine thumbed into her mouth. New drinks arrive, blazingly green. Absinthe. She sips from her glass, licks the salt on its rim.

She feels Ilias watching her. He must sense something;

assume, perhaps, a hesitancy of defences. He starts to talk more freely. He's going to write a book. The dream psychology of buildings. Or, the psychology of dreamt buildings. The theory: where you are, inside, outside, where the windows are, it's all significant to the mind. Can a building be entered, is it sealed, grown over, derelict, are the stairs functional or partial, are there clandestine chambers, tunnels, gardens, where are your family members? Everything is meaningful. He makes a good case. But she remains quiet, has entered a separate mood. Do you dream of buildings? Possibly, she says. *Unremembered Dreams* is a book I should write. He nods, confused. This is the truth, though; she has never remembered a single dream. The other night, he says, you were quite restless. I thought perhaps you were dreaming then. She gestures for the bill. Sorry. Indigestion.

At her apartment they lie in each other's arms. The room revolves slowly. The numbing amnesty of alcohol, like a new grace. Ilias falls asleep, snores gently. On the pillowcase, his dark hair looks painted, somehow iconic. He shaves once a month, allows his beard a full growth, then back to scratch. She's seen it three times, this journey from boyhood to manhood. His body scent is something from the earth, wholesome, safe. On his neck, fresh arboreal cologne that reminds her of a line she once read. *I am a forest, and a night of dark trees: but he who is not afraid of my darkness, will find rosebowers*

7

too under my cypresses. It must end. But tonight, there is only the present, these harmless turning moments. Another. And another.

3 a.m. Night's zone of monstrous emptiness, terrors, the intransitive. She moves to the edge of the bed, sits carefully, her feet on the floor, leaning forward. Outside, the wind is up again, less playful now, intuitive, urging. It's like a voice, has the voice's authority and instruction. The numbers on the clock change. She breathes out. In. Out. Like a knife, the pain splits her. She tries not to make a noise, but a muted blurt escapes her mouth. Ilias is face down, stupored; he doesn't wake. She finds herself slipping to the floor, knees folding under, boneless material, a sack of herself. Her chin hits the carpet, there's spittle all round her mouth. She cannot feel her legs. An extraordinary, medieval agony is halving her body, winding her intestines apart. A strong desire to void her bowels and stomach. The pain divides suddenly, forks up towards her shoulders. Pressure charges all along her back, like lightning crouching in the sky. It is unbearable.

She arches up, begins to move away from the bed, towards the window, fingers digging in the carpet. It feels like she is pulling free from a useless section of herself. She could call for help. But her lips are hard as a beak, her mouth full of gristle. She keeps pulling forward, ripping the carpet, strength she did not know she had, as if crawling from a fire, or a collapsing building. Above her, the whole room seems to be alive, made of soft moving skin. Her eyes begin to blur and spill. When she looks back, everything has warped, her legs are far away, severed, joined by a dark red stem of meat. She passes out.

In the doorway, she tells Ilias she cannot see him again. He's a wonderful man who she is sure will do brilliant things – his expression clouds, and she regrets the patronisation immediately. She tries again. There's too much distance. She is sorry, but it's over. Distance? She shrugs. Just differences between us. He is surprised, but maintains composure; there will be no name-calling, no terrible scene. Still, she feels foolish, fraudulent. It all sounds so pat, the language of a serial romantic performer. Look, I'm unreliable, she says. He laughs. That's it? Don't be ridiculous. Please. He puts a hand to her face. Tell me what I did wrong? The submission, the reproach, is excruciating. She feels herself begin to panic and reverse. He's no criminal, and she is sick or possibly going mad. Something has ruptured in her brain and is trickling out. No, she thinks, no. I am this. There's no choice.

After he has gone she takes a walk. Colder currents have arrived from the north. People are in big coats, scarves, boots. Pools of water glisten on the pavement. Scales of debris slide towards the drains. Under her own coat she feels dormant. She tries to concentrate on work, thinks about the shelter. It will be razed to make way for a development of unaffordable new flats. Vast money is behind the scheme, money from abroad, one of the city's Middle Eastern kingpins, or Chinese, or American, no doubt. The city is being auctioned off and there is little she or anyone else can do. She walks without purpose, turns along the river. She watches people, absorbs them as they get close. Men: blunted by years of precedence, stinking of pheromones. The women. Their eyes give it away; their blood rises. They emit. Distress, fear, hope. Echoes of the past. *Quiet, girl. Your mammy's gone. I'll fuck you till you come apart.*

On the fourth night she makes it to the floor below the window, which has been the draw, and which has been left open, an exit, or an entrance. The pain is the same, and the passage along the floor the same, instinctive, effortful, but by fractions systematic. Beyond the hurt, there is a lifting feeling, a sense of the air's shape and consistency. Something immense and powerful might be close, if she believed. The heap of flesh left behind disgusts her, its look, the sealed bowel, the plug of spinal bone, defecation of an old self. The hole, with all its laws and allure, simply a fistula in meat. Again, she loses consciousness, and wakes rejoined, in the former position, tucked over on the floor.

The days become reduced, emptying of meaning. She works. Her name, the firm's name, are helping the case. There might be compensation, but there will be no stay of execution. Worse is the publicity that the staff thought, desperately, would help. The building, a small Edwardian sanatorium between corporate megaliths, has been revealed. Several men have tried to breach the entrance, piggy-backing after entering staff and sending the residents scattering to their rooms. One husband saw the door's code being keyed. Only because a particular guard was on duty was he was stopped. Cantrell – the calm, steroidal massif, ex-boxer, ex-bouncer, who suffered knife injuries on his arm while holding his attacker's ten-week baby behind his back. After a week's surveillance the police have stepped down their presence. When she visits, the place feels primed for disaster, like a stick house on the prairie, a motherless antelope. She works on the case, but she is simply biding.

Nights are the source of the real dynamic. Each one a lesson in emergence, each one bringing her further. Violent alteration, acceptance, discarding. Crawling. Reaching the window. Pulling herself up on to the sill. The air beaten frantically behind her. Until, one night, she is there, holding the frame, her raw torso hovering an inch above it, balanced, the canopy still shipped inside her back, ballistic, keen. This, the sixth floor of the brutalist tower. The gardens below are paved, unsurvivable. Air's theories sweeping stupidly past: vortices, thermals. Her eyes are closed. She cannot be her own witness.

And then, the survival mechanism is overridden. A half push, half forward cast. The last decision of life, and the momentary drop, a first rush, like the waterfall's crest, the brink of climax. For that second, such kinetic beauty, trust in nothingness. Then – a crack behind her, huge and dull and viscose, as the wings extend, unfurl and are filled, begin her flight. Suddenly, the city is far below, turning slowly in relief, roadways, estates and parks, contoured and furrowed and rapidly passing, a new landscape, a map of the hunt.

Only their cries follow her home. Not the bleats of discomfort during, often they are asleep, do not know exactly what is happening, but after, when they wake and are left with the knowledge of reprieve, when they see small patches of blood on the sheet. Their bodies can be entered through the mouth, belly, the hole through which all was created – the product taken out by the tongue's long catheter. It is no more nutrient than grass used as emetic. It does not take long, if they are sleeping on their backs. A minute. Something about her presence paralyses, as an eclipse dulls the hidden world. Rarely do they rouse. At the first sting, their eyes might flutter open in the dark, the whites glowing like phosphorescent eggs. She puts pressure on the mouth, gently returns them to unconsciousness.

Their confliction after – for it is possible to love the issue of a crime, even as the cure delivers – is theirs alone. She leaves the window as she found it, unlocked, cracked, redeploys herself into the night. Their bodies are reset, if not restored. There is never freedom from it. Or brief freedom might be invalidated, if they do not leave him, if they replace him with another of that kind, if they are, again, unlucky victims. But she never visits the same woman twice. What she is, field surgeon, avorteuse, predator, comes with its own invulnerable mechanic, exemption. She is, must be, human-proof.

Such a raucous call. There are so many – she could not have known before. And she cannot find them all. She seeks first the ones who transmit loudest, smell strongest, those who cannot hide and for whom it will be worst. Girls. The girl given animal tranquillisers, shared by seven of them, a lottery of seed inside. The girl found on the estuary bank, inside a suitcase, not able to speak English, who left the hospital before the interpreter arrived, ghosting every camera. The girl who was filmed, and filmed after giving her consent. The girl whose uncle. The girl whose mother's lover.

The girl whose cousin. The girl who jumped from the bridge and was caught by an angel with wings so vast they looked like moons, who was made love to in the sky, and set down by the lion on the bridge, and that lion was no more a lion than a lapdog then. The disabled. The mentally unwell. She is more ruthless with those, no anaesthesia, because if they see her it will not be believed, she will only have slipped from the wards of their minds. Nights of hunting and listening. Finding, entering. And at the end, in the flare of dawn before she gets back to the tower, the whole embryonic mass is ejected from her mouth, like a senators' feast. Always in the same place, territorially – a small, unmanned sub-station with high walls, near the railway line, where the trains pulse and screech and carry negligible cargo.

The first time she finds the man involved is not pure calculation, though why not remove one to prevent ten. It is progression, the honing of skill. She is on a nearby roof, next to a stretch of unlit scrubland, a cropped silhouette, neither mammal nor avian. She watches until he is done. The woman limps home, borrowing the shadows of the gaslit past, mute until she has shut her front door, then she screams, but not so loud the flatmate will hear. He goes back to the bar. How much better the beer tastes. Like it did when he was eighteen. Golden, fletched with barley, like drinking summer. He tells a few jokes to the barman, puts songs on the jukebox, leaves a message on his sister's phone. Happy birthday, you old cow. Bet you thought I'd forgotten.

Outside, he puts on his jacket, which smells a bit of perfume, and starts to walk home. She takes him by the shoulders, swings him up. A fast few miles – while he kicks, while his mind explodes and he messes himself – to a neighbouring district of industrial warehouses and storage containers. She tries to be slow, inflict, she would like to examine inside and know why. But it is too exciting, or instinctive. Hot spray on her wing. She leaves the pile, like something spilled from a bin. The bloodweight affects her flight slightly, she is less balanced. She turns along the river, skims the surface, cleans. It makes the news. The weapon used is unknown. Nothing has escaped the zoo. The next, just before he veers the woman into an alley, she hoists on to a fire escape, drops. Accident. A broken neck. And no post-mortem to reveal the delicately evacuated heart.

She has no dreams. No conscience. But in the mornings her body begins to seem less true. She is not unwell, but her legs tremor and feel cold, their vascular system compromised. She's thinner, has bad breath, the tooth enamel is eroding, beginning to reveal a softer substance underneath. Her phone rings. Clients, old and new, who are transferred to colleagues, while she works solely for the

Haven. The girl with the pale-green eyes watches her when she comes. She's thirteen, give or take, has a mother sleeping upstairs somewhere. She holds the ragged dog to her breastless ribs, like a threadbare familiar. She watches, and doesn't speak. Reminds her. The money, the land registry, though opaquely concealed, is traceable. She finds the name, and of course it is him, Olayan; he owns half the city, his wealth is a black river running through the world. He is beyond any legal reach.

Fewer friends call wanting lunch. They suspect she is involved with someone inappropriate, or having health problems. She seems withdrawn, never goes out after work. Even Ilias, who has left several hopeful messages, stops calling.

Within weeks the shelter is closed, its door chained until the demolition crane arrives. The women disperse; some are moved a hundred miles to other safe houses, overcrowded centres. Two are swept back into old worlds, one overdoses below a bypass, one is tattooed on the notch above her anus – *Пожалуйста* – and put back on the circuit. Cantrell goes with the mother of the baby to Scotland, the western islands, a stolen act of love. It is over.

One night, instead of circling the city, she finds herself passing over the Channel. The sea is black, bladed, strung with small lights – boats like relics, stacked transport ships. High above the sea both landsides can be felt.

The velocity is tremendous; distance another surprise.
Lowlands. Fields of produce. Agricultural order. Towns
of great, distinctive architecture. Forest, and white
serrated mountains, where her blood translates, becomes
a different temperature. Sea, and sea, separated by land
like lovers walled apart. There are so many stars, multi-
tudes, smoky galaxies, black, undiscovered planets.
Finally, desert. She follows the new road between the
dunes, its straight, immaculate tarmac.

Armoured vehicles surround the complex, groves of
solar panels, and on the perimeter, a tall, inwardly sloping fence, as if he knows what enemy the sky might
convey. A mile inside, modular white constructions
begin. Tiled pools, the impossible prized lagoon.
Fragrances rise from the gardens: black tulip, anise. It is
a palace and a fortress. Arid vectors circle to the ground.
The guards don't look up. From military service to this
easy duty, guns like armrests, TV shows playing on
their phones. He is untouchable by name alone, spider
in the globe's rich web.

His residence is in the inner courtyard, deeply placed.
Its rose-glass roof cannot be scaled. She clings vertically
to the wall, unpicks the vacuum sealant, slides the pane.
Space enough inside to stay airborne, even encumbered
by her span. She sweeps the chamber, soundlessly. No
guards, just one servant, an illegitimate, trusted, or

bought, who turns and sees her coming. He presses back against the wall, and vomits, faints. She drills a tidy puncture through his neck, lifts his legs against the wall to speed the let.

Inside are sensors on the ceiling and the floor. The scent of an unknown blossom, white and perfect. Breath. His bed is vast, and he is sleeping at its edge, as if unconfirmed. Dark hair on the pillow. He is beautiful, this prince, robeless, touchable on the altar. Whichever wife, or boy, or gelding, is finished with and gone. He is washed and oiled. The most powerful man in existence, except one. She retracts, and sits beside him for a moment. She could be a guardian, benign grotesque, a saint. If she had been made differently, or if a treaty had been signed somewhere in history, she might never have come. If what happened had not happened. It is so far away, deep in the vein, behind the lens, an animal's memory. She is alone in the village. She has passed through the door of her neighbour's house, and the high bolt has been slid across. She has pulled down her soiled dress and he has gone upstairs to bed. *We'll do that again tomorrow, shall we, before Mammy gets back home?* She has crawled to the dog's bed, where the dog is sleeping, and has climbed in next to it, and put her face on its damp and dirty fur. She's fallen asleep, and has entered her own imagination, a cystic universe, grown by adolescent rage and disgrace; she is waiting for someone to come and help, waiting for herself.

Enough. The alarms are flashing in another room. He is not the reckoned god she wants. She has come half a world away to know what she can do, who is within her grasp. Going west, she surfs the bore of coming daylight. She sleeps on the wing, dropping altitude, waking, and climbing back up, almost to heaven.

Winter. It is colder than it's been for years. Inside the walls of buildings water swells, turns rigid, splitting pipes, displacing bricks. Ceilings collapse with the weight of ice. The trees are black and stiff as railings. Long, productive darkness, but at dawn, and in twilight hours, there are great studios of teal above the city. She continues to administer, to those she didn't reach, couldn't reach, before. In a clinic in the south, a woman waits for the nurse to leave, then turns the baby over on its front, pushes its head down into the mattress of the crib. Warm, and soft as vegetable. It moves, surprises her with its strength. Strong enough to inch up a body to the breast, if the birth had killed her, if they lay inside a cave, still roped. The woman stops. She rolls the baby over and its mouth sucks air. Hasn't got it in her. She sits down in the chair next to the cot, plastic tube between her legs, and reasons. It should be both of them. Tomorrow she will take it to the river. She cries with relief. The baby cries for milk. The woman dozes. She feels a breeze and when she looks the little boy is gone, adopted by the wind.

The city freezes, encased as if in glass. Points on the train tracks fail. All flights are grounded and planes sit in silver ranks along the runway. The refineries fail to transport. No oil. No grit. Blackouts. There is an over-growth of white along the roads. Jackknifed buses, cars pitched into drifts. People must walk or wait it out inside, rubbing up against each other, knowing there is no escape. Those in charge deny and then declare a state of emergency. Regardless, human core, dependent, unadapted, is exposed. She has it all, the greater part of time, the oceanic dark above the world, superiority. She hears, feels; she preens the masses of their disease. A star could be named for her. A blinding, new immacu-late. Epiphany. But no one sees or guesses.

Fission's nocturne: it is painless now, a habit. Scars develop on her back, faint cords of white and grey. Near her shoulder is a small dry hole, incomplete closure, insignificant, but these are the scales. For advance, for primacy: a levelling. Mutability. Glory. Brevity. She eyes the future with no more fear than a hawk its reflec-tion in a pool.

Now.

The village is the same, hemmed in by mountains weep-ing shale, wet, and ferned. Ditches of brown water score the moorland, wells of snowmelt, bracken on the slopes like burning ember. She passes over, twice, leaves no mark on any door. She sails the narrow length of the valley, along its glacial, feudal gash, arcs back again. Below, the church is empty, roof wrapped in plastic to protect it from decay. The barns are empty too, livestock gone to slaughter, farms sold off. The cemetery gates are closed. The river has redirected only inches. The steep field where her life almost ended, where her father lay beneath the wheel, blood forced into half his body's compartments, eyes haemorrhaging, is fallow. The cottage where her mother passed away, and the cottage of the neighbour, are undistinguished, stacked in thick vernacular grey stone. It is here, one valley, in the thousands of the world, that she comes back to. Pulled by cells, eel-blind, brain a small magnetic pit. She can feel each cloud, the breath of the Atlantic, humid in her lungs. And the natal smell lifting, unforgotten – earth and mineral and rain.

Even she cannot approach easily, is tested by the currents. The mountains flow with cold; wind rotors between the summits. When she lands she comes down hard on her hands and the loose skin behind her luffs. Dawn is approaching; green, underwater light struggling in the morning's storm. The trees are unlocked and rock loosely in the ground. Stones and mud. Water's surfaces mirror only cloud. She walks as she can, on her palms, supplicant, survivor, half-sized like a child, up the path to the house, where he is still living, barely, his chest rotting, his hounds dead, just a man who cannot stand from a chair without great effort, whose eyes are stiff with cataracts, and whose memories have not been saved. He will be waking into humanity, into his last day, and the unheated range, the smell of the empty dog bed, and the cold flagstones on the floor. Perhaps to thoughts of her, whichever stir.

So the first dream ends or never started. She stands waiting at his door again, a creature unwhole, a creature so evolved and lethal it might free the earth's hold on the moon. Everything is near and hers. The old man coughing through the wall as the bolt slides open. On the pillow, Ilias's dark hair grows and curls, and she could go back, could wake him up and say, *I am not this*; she could tell him everything, or nothing, because the present is in each millionth moment remade and unstoppable, forgiveness, war, cause, cure, all moments, all selves, possible. But she is here. This time, she does not put herself away, but lays the wings behind her, as far as they will reach, across the garden, and the fields, almost to the fells, and they are open to the sky, already hardening in the light.

The Woman The Book Read

Ara. The name was unusual; he wouldn't have recognised her otherwise. If she'd walked past him in the street, even if she'd been sitting opposite him in the cafe and he'd had time to study her, he probably wouldn't have guessed. He was at his usual table, taking coffee, reading, watching the gulets dock in the harbour and unload passengers. It was still hot, his sleeves were rolled, but the town dogs were no longer collapsed in the shade – they were up and wandering. End of season, everything had slowed, and there was a sense of recovery, exhalation almost. He didn't care for summers now; each year the town's capacity felt breached. Loud music on the beach platforms, expensive drinks. The proposed airport had been halted, but more people kept arriving regardless.

He was waiting for Eymen, as usual. They were supposed to discuss profits, tax, new ideas for the company, cider import, stonecrop export. Every Wednesday, the same. Eymen would arrive late, sweating, breathless, and would tease him for drinking espresso. You're the late one, old wolf. When are you going to arrive home? If he'd been fiddling with his notebook and pencil he would put them away before they were seen and commented on.

Someone close to the Great Han shouted her name across the square, and his head snapped up instinctively. It took a moment to register. He hadn't heard it spoken in – how long? The name was called again. The accent was unmistakably English. Twenty metres away was a woman in a fedora and a lime-coloured dress – the caller.

The square was less crowded than the previous week. Small groups were congregated by the ice cream stall. The almond seller was talking to an elderly couple in matching linens. The rich young things from the city had gone. The sun was low; the woman in the green dress had her hand cocked, shielding her eyes. She was facing west, towards the lion's tomb. There were two women in her line of sight – one small in stature with bleached hair, another Chinese. By the water's edge Cemile teyze was bent over the dock, mooring *The Domina* after the day's last tour.

Again, the call came, floating across space, like the invitation of a ghost. Ara! Something released in his chest. A sense of her. That familiar feeling: uncomplicated, tender. He'd loved her name; it sounded stateless, when such ideas had seemed possible. *The bringer of rain*: her mother's idea. He knew Catherine had been bullied by the father's family, pressured to change it, even after the birth certificate; he'd admired her stubborn refusal. Whenever he'd thought of Ara, and he so often had – her hand in his, her skin immeasurably soft – he'd imagined she would be doing extraordinary things. She would have flown so far, her time with him forgotten. But if she were here, wouldn't it be because of him? Or was it simply coincidence? The town was popular now, the country stable, and the British especially were building villas all over the peninsula and up into the hills.

The caller was balanced on her toes, waving and gesturing. Come here. He put his hands on the table, next to his coffee cup, and strained upwards to see who was being summoned. A woman was walking round the low wall of the fountain. She'd been drinking from the tap, perhaps, bent to the waterspout, hidden from view. Now she was walking across the square towards the han. Tall – and fair, yes – but the sun was obscuring her face. Her hair was bound back. How strange, his heart's agitation, as if a piece of him already knew.

She arrived out of the late-afternoon light, and he could see she was the right age and had a wide, clear face. She was wearing sunglasses, large and fashionably angled. He couldn't see her eyes. She was scanning the vicinity. If she cast her gaze further left, she would see him. Or she would see a man sitting at a cafe table. He was not unchanged. Nor was he unlike his younger self. Stomach, OK, a little rounder. Hair still good, thick and dark, attractive to women, he knew. The pallor from ten years in her country had disappeared. Bones, of course, were an indication. His were distinctive, slightly leonine, and would probably not begin to sink for another decade. She was beautiful, he could see that – more so, a woman now. The white dress sailed from her body as if she were a rigged ship. Rose-gold skin – so easily burned. When they'd been here before, she'd kept to the shade, struggled at midday. They had retreated back to the hotel often.

Where have you been, he heard the friend ask. Laughter. An apology. Her voice was too low to make out the words. They conversed for a moment. Which one, the friend said. Hurry up, I really want to swim. They both turned and looked at the towels hung and stacked on tables outside the emporium. So many colours – not the best quality, but eye-catching. Her hand brushed over the sky, lavender, turquoise cottons. Should he go over and say hello? How would she feel about that? The last time he'd seen her, at the train station, the tears, the fight – he didn't want to think of it.

A shadow fell across the table, and someone loomed in front. Crumpled trousers, a dark patch along the shirt above the belt. Drinking coffee, I see, foreigner. Who is president of this country? Eymen was fishing in his pockets for some item, elbows flapping, thoroughly obscuring the view. Ah, still so hot, can you believe it. Must be thirty at least, old wolf! Where is the car key? I thought I put it. He leaned to the side to see round his partner, but Eymen was ample, planetary almost. Please get your ass out of the way, Arab. He put his hand on the solid hip, shoved Eymen to the side. Hey! What?

She was gone, inside the han, or away into the square. He still hadn't seen her properly. Eymen was sitting down now, scraping the feet of his chair noisily, complaining about the heat again, he couldn't find parking, why was traffic so bad, there should be a congestion charge for people north of Izmir. Have you ordered my tea yet? He did not reply and Eymen held up his hand for the waiter. He looked towards the marina, the steep street that led to Derya beach. The fountain again. Nothing. She had vanished, like a figment. What's the matter with you today, wolf? And what's this? Eymen picked up the notebook from the table, flapped it. Don't tell me, the master plan? Very carefully, very calmly, as if defusing a bomb or handling a snake, he reached over and removed the pad from his partner's hand. It's my letter of resignation, Arab. He slipped the notebook into his shirt pocket.

The two women emerged from the arch of the han, carrying thin plastic bags along with their totes. It had been a quick transaction, no browsing, and probably carried out in English. He felt a little pinch of sadness. Had she forgotten? They began to walk in the direction of the beach platforms. She had her back to him and the sun flooded her hair, making it seem colourless, then copper, blonde, ash. Like tweed, he remembered Catherine once describing it. He heard the sound of a brush passing through the length of it, once, twice, an exquisite, gentle, tearing sound. How quickly the past could be restored.

He stood abruptly. I have to go. He put some coins down on the table. What? I just arrived. I've got the figures. But already he was walking away. He heard Eymen swearing. Are you coming back? He held up his hand: maybe. Ah, so secretive! Is your new boss a woman?

They were at the edge of the square. He tucked his shirt in as he walked. The feeling was incredibly strong, physical almost. Wanting to see her. No, it was that other feeling, her leaving, pain like a seizure in the chest muscle. He could have said something – Eymen knew about her, of course. But he didn't want any questions, the difficult ones that would surely come, and the uncomfortable silence. They were walking quickly, obviously keen to have their swim before evening. Was it the first? Had they arrived only today? He remembered so well that moment of anticipation, of revelation, when he had been a visitor too. Meeting the sea, having journeyed the length of the country, or further.

The sun was moving behind the peninsula, firing the trees. Shadows were already pitching over the surface of the water. He remembered her excitement when she'd first seen the water's colour here, borrowing light and the sky's blues, so different from the dull zinc of the North Sea. Like a kingfisher, she'd said, and later, back in England, she'd found a picture to show him in a book. It looked right, a creature of extraordinary blue flame. Ten years, and he never saw one, though he looked for them by the rivers.

He followed them past Ruhi Bey, Mavi, the military station. He nodded to Eren in the kiosk but didn't stop to chat, and Eren held up his hands in mock offence. The women talked as they walked, brushing shoulders occasionally – they seemed like fine travelling companions. He followed at a distance that didn't seem intentional or disrespectful, but still he felt ashamed at the stealth. He could easily have caught up, said her name, presented himself. It's you, my goodness, hello! Enough time had passed, everything forgiven, surely. But he held back, padding after her.

That same sensation, of wanting to hold her. She'd been a restless soul, would often shrug him off. *Küçük kuş.* He'd loved teaching her words, little phrases. Sentences were harder, she didn't understand the order of syntax, but then neither had he at first, in reverse. Spiced carrot juice, yoghurt dishes; he'd been irrationally

29

pleased every time she tried them, as if they were con-
necting. Most of all she'd loved sunflower seeds, the ordinary brand, setting aside the ones with shells too difficult
to open. That year with her, he'd gone so many times to
the little trade shop, made a show of pulling the packets
from his bag.

The women paused, took their bearings, and turned
towards Derya. Down the long steps, past the citrus
trees, heavy with old fruit. He saw her glance up at the
branches. When they'd come together – the three of
them, almost a family – it had been late spring and the
lemon flowers were blossoming, their zest climbing
high, white and sweet. Only half the restaurants had
been open, and the sound of hammering had echoed
round the town as hotels and boats were repaired.
Paradise, half my happiness, he had described it.

He'd been coming since university and wanted to show
the place off. Every year, hitchhiking the length of the
country, camping, cheap hostels, then hotels; he'd come
even when flights from England were expensive and it
was hard to get away from work. Wondering who owned
the big shuttered houses behind the harbour, with regal-
looking pomegranates and vines in their gardens. He'd
said even then he would retire here. After the accident,
after Ara had left, everything had felt lesser, or greater.
The rain. The politics. Regret. Abandonment seemed like
a doorway that became a corridor of doorways, easy to

pass through. It hadn't taken long to make the decision to sell the business and return.

The women stopped at the parrot's cage, talked to the bird, tried to get it to speak. It was Aslan Bey's pet, the same one they'd seen so many years before. An African grey. It would outlive them all, probably. Their shoes clopped softly on the white stone path as they continued down. In Derya the sunbeds were mostly empty, umbrellas either retracted or flapping gently in the breeze. The music had moved to a mellower set. One or two last bathers were going into the cubicles to get dressed, people were sipping beer at the bar and smoking. They chose a section on the lowest wooden platform, overlooking the breaking waves, laid their towels out on the loungers. He stood one level up, near a pillar, where he could watch discreetly. The women spoke to the attendant, who did not charge them this late in the day. The attendant lingered, moved one of the parasols a fraction, fussed over the position of their loungers, was flirting, perhaps, then took their order, glancing at him on the way to the bar. He would order a beer if asked.

He leaned on the wooden support and watched them. They were sitting, looking out to sea. She'd taken a book from her tote. It was large, a hardback. She slipped the fastening from her hair and shook it out. For a moment it spilled everywhere, a shining mess. Then she retied it. He remembered one of the many fights he'd heard about. Her father had wanted it cut off, for some stupid reason. He'd tried not to dislike the man; he'd shaken his hand the few times they'd met, and they hardly ever saw him – he worked in a hospital in another town. He had dismissed Catherine when Ara was a baby, and only occasionally made demands. Ara's hair was beautiful. He wondered if her father had prevailed, if she had ever worn it short. Ever dyed it. He wondered how she'd lived, what levels of happiness had been possible. The guilt began to rise.

She took off her sunglasses, set them down on the low table. She turned to the side so he could see her profile. Could he be sure? She was looking towards the island, the vanishing wake of the ferry. He still had a photograph of her, holding the mooring rope of the boat they'd taken out to the sunken city, pretending to pull it ashore. Her big hat shadowing the sweet curve of her nose. He'd transferred it from phone to phone, between laptops. The attendant came back with an order of coffee, elaborate silver cups, dusty sweets on a wooden plate, the full works, not how it was usually served here. It seemed to be the friend he was interested in most, though he was being polite to both, refusing the payment offered. Good, he thought, leave her alone. He could feel his phone vibrating in his trouser pocket. It stopped, then after a moment vibrated again. Eymen. He ignored it. Truly, he did feel doglike, stalking, as if hungry for scraps. Just go to her, he thought.

He stepped forward, put his hand on the railing. She took a sip of coffee, another, admired the cup and set it down. She stood. She pulled a bathing suit from her bag and said something to the friend, who nodded, collecting hers. They skirted the rows of sunbeds and went into a cubicle together. A minute later they emerged, laughing. She had on a dark-red suit, a colour that was unexpected. Her skin looked paler against it, lunar. They stowed their dresses and shoes under the loungers. Her limbs were long, her body compact, the hemlines of the bathing suit sat demurely, while her friend wore a green bikini that revealed more, and was full-figured, what he'd always thought of as his type. The friend clapped her hands together. They laughed again and went down to the diving platform and the sea ladders, dropping out of view.

He moved forward, took the steps down to the next level. He caught the look of the attendant, who was removing the coffee cups. He shook his head, cut the air with his hand, and the young man retreated. Her book was lying on its cover, the pages flicking in the wind. When he looked over, she was facing his way and his stomach lurched. Her eyes slid away almost immediately. She turned to face the water. The waves were moderate. The roped buoys of the swimming lane lifted and lowered. They were trying to decide whether to climb down the ladders, jump or dive, he imagined. Six feet of air in between was not insignificant; Derya always divided the cautious from the brave. How had she done it before?

The friend pointed. The head of a turtle had breached, just beyond the cordon. There was a green-grey shadow where its shell sat under the surface. A few biters had been around recently. Eymen had been got on the calf, quite an impressive welt, a red half-moon and a round of precautionary antibiotics. This could give him reason; he might warn her. But still he did not move. The beaky head popped up and down a few times and then the turtle disappeared. The women turned to each other. They kissed briefly on the lips. Then they kissed again, longer. Ara brought her hand gently to the other woman's face. It was an unmistakable gesture. Intimate, sexual.

Maybe he wasn't surprised. In the years of life that really mattered, men had failed her. Kindness was one thing; he knew he'd always been kind. Love flooding the right chambers: that was undeniable. But those questions, of definition, roles, commitment – those questions demanded everything. What had he given? This was ego, of course; he was indulging himself. You were born with attractions. Her mother had said something once, hinted. It had been here, fooling with coffee grounds and fortunes on the Lycian tour, while Ara was talking to an older girl on the boat. His reading, he remembered, had been indistinct, roads. In the bottom of Catherine's cup – a small black storm, grains shaping a car.

He was beginning to feel cold, though the sun still had strength. It would not really be cold until November. The two women were about to dive and he was thinking of the North Sea, the time he'd swum in it, the almost electrical shock as a wave broke over his back, shingle pouring up his shins as the sea retreated, then stumbling over, flailing rigidly in the water. Even the salt had tasted different, denser, caustic in the eyes and nose. Here, he could swim for hours. The heat reached to the bone. But he was cold, as if this was the season of another country, as if he was opening the door on that autumn night, to the hard wind and rain, the news. If he'd had longer, maybe, or if he and Catherine had married, he could have made a decision that would have mattered in the end. Maybe he could have run with Ara. But everything had happened out of order, too fast, and the lines, no, the law, had been made clear to him.

He found himself half-kneeling, half-sitting on a lounger, an awkward position he did not understand, couldn't adjust. The friend, the lover, jumped. She tucked her legs in and neatened her splash. After a moment under water she reappeared, face to the sky, her hair slicked back. It's warm, come in! Ara waited a moment, then she dived, cutting the water vertically,

35

like a dropped knife. It was an incredibly graceful movement; so adult. She was gone, deeply, barely any foam. Ten seconds, fifteen – long enough that he felt a flurry of panic. She surfaced. Her girlfriend said something, seemed impressed, perhaps it was the first time she'd seen that. They swam round each other, floated on their backs, then swam out to the cordon, resting their arms along the rope.

Fearless. Adept. Is this who she had become? He wanted to know everything, every detail. What she liked to eat, what she had studied, if she had studied – she must have, she'd been clever – the music she listened to, whether sadly or dancing. Which moment had she realised what death meant, and who had comforted her, brought her water when she was sick. Whether she had taken her driving test, whether she hated cars. Could she sing, paint, did she believe in a god? Did she remember him? He wanted to open her bag and rifle through it for clues. Or just sit and wait for her to come back, try to embrace her, say he was sorry. And tell her, though perhaps it was unspeakable, and she must already know, that she looked like Catherine.

It was impossible. He couldn't go to her. He didn't exist any more. She could easily have found him, if she'd wanted to, if she'd come to this town as anything other than a tourist. Reunion was easy these days, even after so much time. And she didn't exist either, not this grown version. What existed was the first perpetual story – a girl, four years old, who had, sometimes, to his discomfort and pleasure, called him *Baba*. The smell of apples in her shampooed hair as she kissed him good-night. Her little plimsoles on the station platform, walking away from him and towards her father, not understanding this wasn't just a visit with a man she hardly knew, a stranger, who now had every right to keep her. As she'd mounted the train she had suddenly begun to cry and struggle, realising something was wrong, and she'd been lifted aboard quickly and disappeared. Before going to the station, he had tried to explain about the accident, the weather, how people sometimes ended, but she hadn't understood. I can still see Mummy tomorrow? He had tucked things into her bag, snacks, her favourite soft toy, and written an address, though she couldn't read yet. Her father he'd taken by the collar, pushing him hard up against the train. He'd said nothing, nothing meaningful. Just a few words in his first language the man couldn't understand. And then he'd walked away.

What surprised him most was how quickly Catherine had become the past. Like posting a key back through a letterbox. Like turning out the bedroom light. Shock, and hurt, yes. But the wound of lovers lost was seldom fatal – he understood. Ara, though, was alive, and gone, and his love remained unspent. Work – God, how he had worked after. Almost to the point of empire, almost to the point of collapse. He was single, successful, still had occasional girlfriends, a house on the road near the ancient theatre, an orchard with wild splitting fruit; he was a man who'd conquered England, they said, even if they teased him about his habits. He'd never married, never settled. But his life had not felt childless.

The currents must be warm out there – the women showed no signs of swimming back, even though the light was fading. The attendant was by the bar, having a cigarette. The evening prayer would start soon over the loudspeaker. Eymen would be fuming. Most likely, he had left the cafe and gone into the han, to play backgammon with Kenan. He stood stiffly and jogged back up the beach steps. Aslan Bey, the owner of Derya, was feeding the parrot. He greeted him but did not stop. One exceptional, rude day after twenty years of courtesy; surely that was allowed?

At the top of the steps he turned towards town and ran along the street until he got to the kiosk. Eren's youngest son had taken over for the night, a low-lidded boy who spent too long making the right change. He scanned the stocks, bought a cheap packet. He ran back down the road to Derya, passed Aslan again and the attendant; they must have thought him mad, and perhaps he was. He moved through the loungers, to the edge of the lower platform. The sea was sapphiric, empty.

They were coming dripping up the steps from the shower. There was no time to hide. He moved to the side to let them pass. Pardon, he said. He looked at her. She glanced at him, thanked him, and smiled. Her eyes were exactly Ara's. *Küçük kuş*: he almost said it. He stood still, waiting, feeling as hard and exposed as the tombs along the hillside.

The women passed by, collected their towels and dresses, and went to the cubicle, leaving dark wet footprints on the walkways. He made sure the door was shut and moved to their loungers. Someone – the attendant, probably – had turned her book over to stop it from spoiling, marking a page that the wind had chosen with a paper napkin. The title was complicated. There was a diagram of a man on the cover, and the organs inside the chest were visible. A medical journal of some kind. Perhaps she was a doctor, like her father. The thought did not make him unhappy. He lifted the book and placed the sunflower seeds underneath, then turned and walked quickly back up the steps and away from Derya. They were the ordinary brand, unshelled, so her fingers wouldn't struggle.

The Grotesques

If she'd been someone else, the prank might have seemed funny. The vagrant Charlie-bo, who was quite famous around town, a kind of filthy savant, was lying on his back in his usual spot under the shop awning. He was asleep or passed out. Perhaps he was even dead, Dilly couldn't tell. A mask of fruit and vegetables had been arranged over his face to create another awful face. Lemons for eyes – the pupils drawn in black marker pen. A leering banana smile. Corncobs were stacked round his head as a spray of wild hair. The nose – how had they done it? – was an upright slice of melon, carved, balanced, its orange flesh drying and dulling. It was all horribly artistic. Dilly stood close by, staring. The face was monstrous and absurd, like one of the paintings in the Fitzwilliam. There was a make-shift palette of newspaper under Charlie-bo, and his feet and hands were upturned and huge. He wore as many layers as a cabbage, and over the holey, furling garments, that enormous grey gown, a cross between a greatcoat and a prophet's robe, tied with a pleated cord.

Dilly hadn't meant to stop; she was late getting home with Mummy's shopping. But the scene was too terrible. People were walking past, bustling around her. Some were making unkind comments. *Good God, look at the state.* There had even been a few laughs, and some clapping, as if this were a street performance. It might have been art, but Charlie-bo hadn't done this to himself; Dilly knew that. He was so far gone, a wreck of a man, a joke already. He lumbered around town and could barely speak. Often he was prostrate in a doorway, drunk. The prank must have been carried out in daylight – brazenly. She could hear an internal voice, Mummy's voice: *disgraceful, who are these wretches?*

Students, that was who. They were back after the summer break, spoiled from Mediterranean sailing and expensive capital apartments, or loafing on their estates, whatever they did. There had been several esoteric japes in the city since their return. A Halloween mask and nipple-peep bra had been placed over one of the stone saints outside St Giles. The Corpus Clock had been defaced, its glass shield painted with an obscene image, so the rocking brass insect looked like it was performing a sexual act – having a sexual act performed on it, actually. Edward had seen and reported back to Mummy, who was outraged and still talking about it, even though she had no association with the college, or any of the colleges.

Edward had seemed rather amused, but quickly sobered in solidarity. First-term antics. Once the Gowns arrived back, they imperiously reclaimed the town, before settling in and getting on with their studies.

Poor Charlie-bo. It was really too much. He wasn't a statue on a church. Dilly wanted to kneel down and remove the ridiculous fruit, shake him awake, help him to his feet. Perhaps if she did, Charlie-bo would revert to his old self, smile and speak articulately, as he hadn't for years. He would thank her. Those reddened, free-roaming eyes would hold her gaze, kindly, shyly. Something spiritual would pass, perhaps – a blessing story, like those Father Muturi had preached about last Sunday. Dilly lifted her hand, paused. The lemon pupils were looking right at her. Charlie-bo's coat was grimy, lined by the dirty tides of the street, and there was a strong, crotchy smell. *Silly girl,* she heard Mummy say. *Don't be so squeamish.*

Mummy was right, of course. She usually was. She could immediately detect faults, like recoil and embarrassment, in her children, even if she couldn't find her own purse or shoe, or she'd lost the car, or a bit of bacon grease was in her hair, making it rear up. Dilly sometimes thought that Mummy was like a truffle pig, rooting around and unearthing ugly, tangled thoughts in people. She especially did not like shame or reticence. You had to stride into a room; wear any dress, day or

43

night, like you were at a gala event; speak to strangers without inhibition. *Just have a go, Dilly, for goodness' sake. Engage!* By now, Mummy would have swept the degrading parody face away and helped stand Charlie-bo up, with that superhuman little woman's strength of hers. Even if he were dead, she would have the power to resurrect him. She would buy him a cup of tea in Jarrold's. Then she'd tell the story, marvellously, afterwards.

Dilly put her hand back in her pocket. Without warning, Charlie-bo flinched. He jolted, as if struck by an electrical current. The melon tipped over, and a lemon rolled from his eye socket on to the pavement, quite near Dilly's foot. Charlie-bo grunted, reached up and groped at his head. He looked like someone on the television coming round from an operation, trying to remove tubes. The banana and corncobs fell away and the real face was revealed: discoloured skin with reefs of eczema and cold-burns, a sore, sticky mouth.

Charlie-bo kept patting his head, making panicked, bleating noises. His eyes – Dilly hadn't been this close to him before – were a mad yellowish-green. There were watery cysts in his eyelids. His gaze was trying to find purchase on something. The striped awning. Sky. Her. He sat up. He flailed an arm out, brushed Dilly's skirt, and blurted a sound that seemed fatty and accusing. Dilly took a step backwards. She shook her head. *No,* she thought. *I wanted to help.* Charlie-bo was looking at her, and through her. He made another attempt to speak. His tongue was oversized, a giant grub inside his mouth. She took another step backwards, and a cyclist tinged his bell in warning and flew past. Someone bumped her hard on her thigh with the corner of a shopping bag. Dilly turned and began to walk away.

Behind her, she could hear Charlie-bo making loud, obscene noises. She sped up, weaving round pedestrians. He might be up on his feet now, lumbering after her. *It wasn't me*, she thought. *Please please please.* She half-ran towards the punt station and Queen's Bridge, her heart flurrying. She passed Lillian's boutique. The door was open and she thought someone said her name, but she kept her head down. Before she turned the corner by the wine merchant, she cast a look behind, expecting to see him, his cloak flying, his face hideous with rage. But Charlie-bo wasn't there. She came to a stop by the river, feeling woozy with relief.

The towpath was quiet, just a few people walking and cycling. She went a little way along and sat on a bench, waited for her nerves to calm. The river was a rich opaque green. Leaves from the chestnut trees had fallen and were riding along on the surface. The river always made her feel better. It would be lovely to walk that way home, the long way round, watch the swans and the glassy fluid sliding over the weir. But she was probably very late now

45

and Mummy would be getting cross. Mummy had only sent Dilly out for a few items – teabags, cream, jam. It had taken a long time to decide on the jam. Dilly couldn't remember if Mummy had asked for a particular kind, and she'd begun to fixate on the seeds in the raspberry jam jar. They'd seemed like a million prickly eyes.

People were coming over to the house for a little get-together that afternoon – it was Dilly's birthday, actually, though the fact kept slipping her mind. Father Muturi, who was Mummy's favourite priest at St Eligius, was coming, and Cleo and Dominic, of course, possibly Peter if he finished work in time, not Rebecca, obviously, though Dilly still sometimes forgot, and a lady was coming who could perhaps help Dilly get a job at a magazine, on the arts column. Dilly had wanted to ask Sam, but it was beginning to look like Sam didn't meet with anyone's approval. He'd been a bit too quiet at the dinner last week, and hadn't wanted to sing when Mummy had asked him to. When Dilly had sung her number, a northern sea shanty, which she'd performed nicely but with the usual mild mortification, Sam had looked suddenly very frightened. He hadn't replied to Dilly's last three messages. And he hadn't been to their French evening class this week.

Mummy was making scones for the tea party, which was quite a production; things would be getting tense at home, even though scones, as far as Dilly could tell, were not very difficult to make. She should really go. *Get on, Dilly!* She should be thinking of interesting things to say to the lady from the arts magazine, and sorting her face out. But the river was so smooth and lovely. It felt very receptive. She'd walked along it with Rebecca in the summer, on a very hot day, and had tried to say kind things. She'd said that, as Peter's little sister, she knew him as well as anyone did, and, even if he seemed a bit *other*, she was sure he did care. It wasn't a disloyal thing to say, she'd hoped. Rebecca had been crying on the walk, silently, her face was soaked, her unwashed hair pulled back under a headband, and she hadn't replied. Rebecca had cried a lot last summer, because of the baby. And because of Peter, though Mummy maintained Peter had done nothing wrong, that he couldn't take leave from work willy-nilly, and that Rebecca had been crying to *a worrying degree* and might be becoming *a rather diffi-cult character*. It was hard to know what to think about it. Or feel about it. Dilly had written a few letters to Rebecca, but had thrown them away. It couldn't be spo-ken about, unless raised by Mummy, and then certain agreements were made.

A good party story to tell would have been how she'd helped Charlie-bo, how she'd intervened, stopped the ridicule. It was so hard to make yourself the hero of your stories, be witty but still seem humble – Mummy and Cleo were masters at that kind of thing.

Dilly looked downstream. It was the usual scene. Houseboats with bicycles mounted on their sides. Joggers. The metal bridge – Sorrell's – the only ugly bridge in the city. There were some newly built houses with chalet-style balconies that Edward liked. Who lived there, she wondered. Different people. The common opened out, and the river trickled away to nothing on the horizon.

She became aware of a light rain falling. Her skirt was damp and the towpath now had a leaden sheen. The swans were tucked away, heads under their wings, holding so still in the current they could be pegged underwater. She'd forgotten to take an umbrella from the house, of course. Her hair was difficult if the rain got it for too long, *unmanageable*, which would be a problem later. She stood and began to walk back towards the punt station. The drops were already getting heavy; she could feel them trickling on her forehead and round her eyebrows. The punts were parked in a row, hooded and chained. Four or five people were looking over the edge on the bank opposite, up above the weir. One person was pointing. Something was probably caught in the froth at the bottom of the water's curtain. It was one of Mummy's peeves, all the junk being tossed into the river – riparian fly-tipping, she called it. Suitcases, bin bags, toasters. Almost as bad as the uncleared dog mess and barbecue scorches on The Green.

Dilly didn't have time to stop and look. She turned, walked over Queen's Bridge and continued up the road, past the charity shop, which always had lovely blouses on its mannequins, past The Blue Bell, towards Monns Patisserie. Monns was very difficult. There was a kind of pastel, underworld glory to the window. The cakes were tormentingly delicious, with such delicate architecture and sugar-spun geometrics, candied fruit, chocolate curls. She often found herself gazing at them and getting lost. It was best not even to look. But she couldn't help it. Today, the cakes seemed so perfect and beautiful that she began to feel emotional. Her throat hurt. She wanted to sit down on the pavement and hold her knees.

She was hungry; that was it. An egg for breakfast was all Mummy had allowed, no toast because Dilly was currently off carbs. Lunch hadn't seemed to materialise. Instead, there'd been a little debate about what to wear to impress the lady from the magazine. Several skirts were rejected, and there had been a lot of frustration in the room. Mummy and the lady, her name was possibly Marion or Beatrice, had fallen out a few years ago over something written in an article. Now they were friends again. That was not uncommon with Mummy's acquaintances.

One of the cakes in Monns seemed to have a waterfall of glittering cocoa powder on its edge, almost hovering, suspended in the air. How had they done that?

Perhaps her eyes were blurring in the rain. *Do buck up, Dilly.* Soon there would be scones, Mummy's speciality: warm, soft, comforting, with cream and jam. It might be possible to slip an extra one on to her plate unseen. There was an art to second helpings: you had to be confident and move fast, look as if you were helpfully clearing crockery. Dilly wondered if Charlie-bo was hungry. There was the question of alcohol, which might take priority. Of all the homeless people in town, Charlie-bo was best known, cherished even. He'd been a student at the university, studying Heidegger, or the eleventh dynamic of space, something very avant-garde and awfully difficult. He'd been in contention for a Nobel, people said. Mummy maintained Charlie-bo was from a small northern village, just like her – an unbelonger, a bootstrapping scholarship boy. Too much studying, or a drug trauma, or a stroke – some calamity had done for him, and he'd begun his descent. For a while he'd been a brilliant celebrity of the streets and shelters, until his mind dissolved. A casualty of genius. At least, that was the story.

By the time she got to Northumberland Road, Dilly felt wet and dizzy. The rain had done a very thorough job. Her hair stuck to her temples. The bottom door of the house was locked – its key had been missing for a while – which meant she wouldn't be able to slip in unnoticed. She trudged up the steps to the front door and through the window saw Father Muturi in the lounge, standing at the fireplace and talking to Edward. Father Muturi liked to stand by the fire and say how cold England was. He would say things like African children learned to walk younger because it was warmer there.

If Edward had been called down, Dilly was very late. She waited outside for a moment, very close to the front door, perhaps only an inch from it. She could feel her breath against the wood. The smell from her mouth was like pickle. She could see cracks in the red paint. Inside one was the tiniest insect – its legs poking out, awkwardly. She put her hand on the knob. She took it off again. Sometimes doors could seem impossible. Impossible to open. Impossible to walk through. She felt as if she was the door, as if her own body was shut. Her hair was wet and stupid. Her coat was dripping. *Lordy! Have you been for a dip at the river club, Dilly?* She could hear cars on the street, the squealing brakes of a bicycle as it slowed at the bottom of the hill.

Recently, Mummy had arranged a session with Merrick, the psychoanalyst who lived at number 52, to talk about things like this, and give Dilly 'a bit of a boost'. *You can tell me anything you like*, Merrick had said. *Anything about anything.* It had seemed almost like a riddle, the way he'd said that. *Should we start with why you came back from London?* Merrick had been

51

wearing terrible socks with orange diamonds on the ankles, perhaps in an ironic way. It was strange seeing him away from Mummy's parties, where he was usually dancing, or flirting with Cleo. His practice was in the basement of his own house, and Dilly could see the shoes and legs of people walking past on the street above. She even saw the red-tipped, winking underparts of a dog. The furniture wasn't leather; it was suede, mustard colour. There was a painting on the wall that was abstract but looked like a woman with a whirlpool in her stomach. Was it supposed to look that way, Dilly had wondered, or did it look like different things to different people? Was it, in fact, a kind of test?

Dilly had prepared things to say to Merrick, all very carefully thought through, but she hadn't said much in the end. *After my bag was stolen, I didn't feel very safe in London.* The truth was, no single cataclysmic incident had occurred. It was more a series of daily stumbles, problems she couldn't solve alone. The forgetting of meals, not forgetting exactly but being defeated by so many options, and rent payments, not making the milk convert to perfect, solid foam in the cafe where she worked. Merrick had looked rather sceptical and bored for most of the hour, then, towards the end, disappointed. He'd finished the session with a little talk about boundaries and identity within a family, he'd used a fishing-net metaphor, and Dilly had felt uncomfortable and was glad when it was over. Mummy hadn't asked her about the session.

The rain was coming down, pattering, darkening the pavement. She would be spied any moment, by Edward or Father Muturi. The scones couldn't be served until the jam and cream, which were in the bottom of Dilly's bag, had been delivered. Mummy liked Dilly to make up the tea tray for guests, using the Minton set. Dilly couldn't exactly explain her lateness; she never could. It was, it would be, more a question of absorbing the annoyance. Letting Mummy's words come into her without feeling them. One possibility was to tell the Charlie-bo story; somehow amend it and seem less uninvolved. If she told it interestingly, earnestly, with the beautiful sneer and radio tone of Cleo, or with something approximating Mummy's comedic affront, that might be good enough. She might hold the room. She would, of course, be asked about her level of activity. *Didn't you do anything, Dilly, for goodness' sake?* Perhaps she could say she had done something. Mummy would. Mummy could change a story or revise history with astonishing audacity, and seemed to instantly believe the new version.

Edward was waving at her through the window, mouthing *door's unlocked,* which of course it always was, even when they all went off on holiday. She pushed it and stepped into the hallway. There were voices in the lounge, Edward's affable small talk, and Father Muturi's lovely Kenyan laugh. *I just need to take these*, she called. She heeled off her boots and went very quietly downstairs to the kitchen. Ghost steps: she was an expert. From the kitchen came the gorgeous, golden smell of baking. The table was in chaos, bowls of spilling flour and dribbling eggshells, some lilies still wrapped in plastic dumped in a jug. The tea tray was not set up. Mummy was turned away, bent over the open oven. There was a white handprint of flour on her skirt. She had on fishnet tights and heels, which meant Dilly would have to find a pair of heels too.

The scone smell was almost unbearable. She was so hungry. If she could have just an apple before trying to make polite conversation with the lady from the arts magazine, things might be OK. But the fruit bowl was empty except for a glove. Mummy was naturally slight and trim. Her children were all taller and heavier, like their father with *broad Dutch genes*, and their intake had to be watched. Daughters, anyway. Peter and Dominic were allowed to finish the roast when they were home, then play tennis afterwards to work it off, while the girls cleared up.

The oven fan was whirring. Classical music was playing on the stereo. Mummy hadn't noticed Dilly; she was busy flapping the scones with a tea towel. Her hair was spilling from its blonde nest. Dilly put her bag quietly down on the table, removed the jam and cream. She placed them behind the flower jug, where it might seem they'd been sitting innocently for an hour, then backed out of the kitchen. She ran upstairs, past the hall mirror – yes, she looked a mess, mascara smudged, lips pale, drowned-cat hair – up to the second floor and into the bathroom. She shut the door, moved the linen basket in front of it. She looked in the bathroom cabinet for a volumiser, some kind of lacquering spray. There was a box of half-used hair dye, magazine sample sachets of face cream, Edward's cologne and an old splayed tooth-brush. Nothing helpful.

Below, the doorbell rang. More party guests arriving, probably, though there were always people coming and going for other reasons. She half-expected to hear Mummy's voice calling up – *Door, Dill-eee* – as if Mummy might sense, might even see, somehow, that she was home. Dilly picked a towel up off the floor, sat on the toilet lid, and rubbed her hair. There was a comb in the bathtub and she scraped it through her fringe, tried to create something chic to one side of her head. She was sure she had a nice lipstick somewhere, a dark, sophisticated red, given to her by Cleo, who was always being sent free cosmetics. It had come in a little metallic sack, and was called something strange that didn't suggest colour at all, but a mood, a state of fortune.

Advantage. Ascent. She sat for a while thinking, but couldn't remember the name.

The lounge was extremely warm when Dilly went in. A furnace of coal glowed in the fire's cradle. There was simmering laughter and conversation, the gentle clanking of cups on saucers. Everyone had arrived: Cleo, Dominic and his wife, Bella, Peter, who was in his officer's uniform, the magazine lady, or at least an unknown lady in a black dress, and some of Mummy's other friends. Dilly tried to enter the room with a combination of subtle grace and moderate drama, to be seen and perhaps admired, but also pass into the throng without much notice or comment. Mummy was beside the table pouring tea into cups on saucers held out by Bella. Bella was very good at helping, and she seemed to have doubled her efforts since Rebecca. Mummy had on a little blonde fur stole and a black cardigan. There was still a faint white flour mark on her skirt. Next to the tea tray sat a plate of perfect, mounded, bronzed scones. The jam and cream had evidently been found and were set out in matching bowls. Dilly was desperate for a scone, but Mummy was right there, so she moved towards Edward, who, more often than not, would give up his plate if he saw a lady without.

As she was making her way round the perimeter of the group, Cleo turned and took hold of Dilly's elbow. *If it isn't the mystery birthday girl,* she said. *What have you been up to? Spying for the government?* She kissed Dilly on the cheek. Cleo smelled heavenly, some kind of antique French talcum, or a salon-grade shampoo. Her hair, tresses and tresses of it, was piled high. She had on a silky maroon item, not a dress, nor a jumper; it draped perfectly from her shoulders and was belted at her waist. Her face was dewy, flawless. *Goodness, you do look beautiful, Dilly, what a fabulous combination, very laissez-faire.* Dilly had put together long, wide suit trousers on loan from Lillian's shop, part of the new winter range, and a pink silk shirt rifled from Edward's cupboard. In her haste to get ready, the combination had seemed a stroke of casual sartorial humour. But when Cleo gave compliments, you could never quite be sure whether there wasn't another message. Cleo lowered her voice, conspiratorially. *Just a moment, there's a tiny bit.* She raised her top lip and pointed to her front teeth. Cleo's teeth were slightly gapped, making her somehow seem both sexual and childlike. Dilly licked around to remove the lipstick. *Thanks.* Cleo tutted. *Bit of a dull crew this afternoon, isn't it?* Her mouth rode upwards. She looked like the most beautiful snarling show dog. *Shame Sam couldn't come. But probably it's not his kind of thing? Let's say hi to the boys.*

Cleo linked her arm through Dilly's and stepped her towards their brothers. Peter and Dominic kissed Dilly on both cheeks and resumed their conversation, which sounded political, something to do with a war in Venezuela. They were disagreeing, amiably. Cleo began a funny anecdote – inserting it elegantly into the discussion – about when she had flown to the wrong airport in Venezuela, the plane landing in a field full of little horses, and getting a lift to Barquisimeto with some chaps who it turned out were not really all that savoury. Peter laughed quietly, uncontrollably; Cleo knew exactly her audience. Dominic looked as if he was gearing up for a story of his own, but he probably knew it wouldn't compete.

The four Quinn siblings, standing together in a group. For a few nice moments, it felt to Dilly like a completed puzzle. It hadn't felt that way for a while, not since things with Rebecca, which Mummy described as *one of the worst things to have happened to the family*, her attachment, her over-attachment, to the baby. Some of the words that had been said, by Rebecca when she was very upset, and also by Mummy, afterwards, had echoed in Dilly's head a long time. *Congenital. Abusive. Your son's twisted priorities and your bloody eugenics – now it's fine to destroy life?* Dilly didn't know how people could believe in exact opposites where humans were concerned. Mummy could be quite fierce about her sons, but sometimes Peter did need their help, actually, where emotions were concerned. It was awful when things, when people, went wrong. It hadn't really happened since their father had left, and that had been Mummy's predominant brown study, until Rebecca. The greatest betrayal of all was to disaffiliate.

Dilly's tummy hurt. There was a sound in her ears that happened when hunger got to a certain stage, a kind of humming generator noise. She could hear Mummy talking loudly, saying something about *that naughty Peter not being in a proper jacket*, though Mummy quite liked it when Peter arrived at Northumberland Road off-duty, in his kit. Dilly kept her eyes busy and away from the zone where their gazes might meet. In a moment Mummy would probably come over, say something remonstrative, and want to introduce Dilly to the magazine lady. There would be one of those rapid, awkward, whispery interrogations about where Dilly had been, *mousing off again,* and then she'd have to pretend to be poised and ready for an interview, which wasn't a proper interview, but a kind of cultural conversation test that might lead to some work, or at the very least to a temporary internship that might lead to some work. Dilly had read the arts section of the papers at the weekend, but couldn't remember anything interesting. She had half an idea for an article about the colour yellow, how yellow was being reclaimed by women after years of being unfashionable. Also colour therapy, how yellow had a certain effect, psychologically, in relation to

mental health. Dilly hadn't quite worked the proposition out yet, but if she started talking, hopefully things
would expand. The room was stuffy and a bit smoky and
she felt sick. It was a dangerous point; she knew that
from the past. She really did have to eat.

She slid out of Cleo's arm, and went over to Edward
and Father Muturi. Father Muturi seemed not to have
moved an inch from his warm spot. *Cleo*, he exclaimed,
I was hoping to meet you! Actually, I'm Dilly, Dilly
said, *that's Cleo there.* She pointed. There was a pause.
Ah yes, Delia. Father Muturi turned to Edward. *She
comes to church a lot, this one. A good girl. Yes, I know*,
said Edward. *That's a splendid shirt, Dilly. I was thinking of wearing it myself.* Edward was smiling, eyes pale
and bright behind his glasses. His face was purplish-
red, which made his hair look extraordinarily white. He
must be cooking inside his wool cardigan. It had taken
a little while, but Edward had got used to the borrowing
arrangements in the house. Only his brown Belstaff
was off-limits. It was very expensive, his favourite coat,
and couldn't be risked, especially as the boys were
known to misplace coats a lot. Mummy sometimes
teased Edward about it, called it his *lucky war corres-
pondent's jacket*, but they seemed to have reached an
agreement.

Father Muturi's plate was empty on the mantleshelf,
but Edward still had half a scone, the bottom piece cut

very cleanly, with no scattered crumbs. He hadn't yet spread anything on top. Dilly willed him to see – to feel – how desperate she was. But Edward seemed slower than usual, or less observant, or perhaps he just assumed Dilly had eaten. Father Muturi was coming to the end of his rotation at St Eligius; he was talking about going home. It would be good to get back to those who really needed him. The English were good citizens, not believers. *Well, we shall be very sad to lose you*, Edward was saying, though Edward in fact did not attend Mass unless it was Christmas Eve and he'd had a few vodkas. The skin on his face looked so red and shiny it might burst. As she listened to them talk, everything felt very light and thin, and Dilly thought how kind it would be to reach up and prick the surface of Edward's skin with a pin. Once, twice, on each cheek.

There was a pause in the conversation. *It's my birthday*, Dilly said. *Today. It's today.* The men looked a bit startled. She had blurted it, really quite rudely. *Today?* Father Muturi said. *It's your birthday?* Dilly nodded. She glanced at the hovering scone plate, the beautifully baked half-wing that Edward wasn't eating. Mummy's laugh whooped out, she'd told a joke, or someone had. *That is very wonderful*, Father Muturi said. *We must do a birthday blessing. Oh, yes, marvellous*, said Edward.

Father Muturi cleared his throat noisily, stepped down

off the hearth and into the room. He was a big man and when he moved it was seismic. The heads of the guests turned. Father Muturi held out his hands. He waited, professionally, horrifyingly, for attention, and Dilly began to realise what was happening, what was going to happen. One by one the guests fell quiet. Mummy's voice was the last to ring, its notes high, its key pervasively major. She stepped round the guests and came closer, positioned herself at the front. Theatre at a party was her favourite thing.

Father Muturi waggled his fingers a little. Edward had removed himself to the side and Dilly was now, inescapably, the main scene. Everyone's eyes were on her, Mummy's especially, a concentrated, avian glare. Dilly tried to smile, to look game, and humble, ready to receive. She glanced at Cleo for help, but her sister was whispering something in Peter's ear and smirking. Dilly looked down at the floorboards. The dizziness was not airy any more, but heavy, located inside her body. She felt like a weight going down into dark water. In London, she had fainted a few times – low on iron – and been given tablets that tasted nasty and turned everything black. It was quite nice, disappearing for a little while. It would be quite nice now. But, of course, there would be the waking, the being helped up, the fuss, and knowing she had been a spectacle, more of a spectacle than she already was.

Father Muturi set his feet wide apart and placed his hands on Dilly's head. She felt her knees bend and she sank involuntarily. The hands followed her down, made contact again. Dilly tried to stay still. She tried to be present, but it did feel as if she was being towed away. The priest began. *On this very special day, this very special girl who God has given . . .* He paused. *How many years, please?* He was asking Dilly, or anyone. *Thirty*, called Mummy. *She's thirty!* Then, as an aside, *Lordy, can you believe it, our Dilly!* There were a few claps, though why Dilly didn't know. The pressure of Father Muturi's touch lifted. He made an um-ing noise, and seemed confused. Dilly shut her eyes, waited. Was this bad? She thought of Charlie-bo. His giant robe-like coat. His ruined hazel eyes. His terrible predicament: not the fruit joke, but his life. She thought of Rebecca, pictured her, fatally, like the painting of the goat in the Fitzwilliam with its red headband, standing in salt near the water, its amber eyes dying. She'd taken Sam to see it a few weeks ago. She'd wanted to tell him that this was what happened when you didn't belong any more, when you took the sins of others and were cast out. Like Rebecca. Rebecca was a scapegoat. It was a secret, dangerous thought, not ever to be shared with anyone. And Sam hadn't really been interested in the painting – he'd wanted to see the Samurai masks. Father Muturi touched Dilly's hair again, gently, firmly, and she

63

thought of the river, the river's grace and indifference. She felt the river moving past her, its strong, cold muscles. She felt herself going with it. After a moment the priest spoke, issued some kind of blessing, but Dilly couldn't really hear.

When it was over, the guests went back to chatting and laughing and drinking tea. Dilly sat down on the sofa. For a moment, she felt Mummy's eyes still on her, assessing, but nothing passed between them. Mummy must have sensed, decided not to make the introduction, because Dilly wasn't hoisted over to the magazine woman. Instead, a cup of tea was handed down to her. And then a plate, bearing a whole, uncut scone, with two glistening heaps, white and red, cream and jam. Around the scone was the faded Minton pattern, a ragged botanical tangle. Dilly felt the corner of one eye dampen. Mummy didn't say anything, but the relief, the reprieve, was overwhelming. Her hands were trembling a little as she pushed her thumbs into the soft body of the scone and split it open. She took one big piece and swabbed it through the jam and then through the cream; she lifted it and bit into it. The ducts at the back of her mouth stung and saliva flooded out painfully. She almost gagged. Then the taste came, sweet, wheaty, that safe, wonderful, family taste. Merrick had been wrong. She had tried to be unmoored, tried to live without protections, but the world was full of grotesque, frightening, ridiculous things. It was full of meaningless sorrow and contradiction. Like a sick little baby, with a perfect soul. Here – didn't he see? – they could all help each other. Failure could be forgiven, good things shared. They could all *be* each other. Who you were, really, was who else you were.

It seemed like a miracle to be left alone on the sofa with tea and food, but there she was. The party continued. Dilly ate the scone quickly, a kind of racked, grateful devouring. She licked jam off her finger. She went to the table and took another scone, heaped on cream – no one saw, no one stopped her – and sat back down with her plate. People were talking, sipping tea, having a jolly time, legs and shoes moved here and there. Her brothers and sister and Mummy circulated. The fire began to die. Father Muturi left, maybe for Kenya. He didn't look at her and he made no goodbyes. The front door closed. A minute later the doorbell rang. Dilly looked up at Mummy to see if she should be the one to answer, but Mummy was already en route, adjusting her pale fur stole. Dilly's duties, it seemed, were all suspended.

She heard a muffled discussion at the door, ladies' voices, ups and downs, trills of indistinguishable words. It was longer than the usual welcome-and-coat-off conversation, so perhaps not a party guest. Then she heard Mummy exclaim, shrilly, *gracious, no!* Mummy came back into the

lounge with Lillian, who must just have closed the boutique. Lillian was carrying the loveliest-looking package,
an immaculate silver box with a huge beige bow, probably
for Dilly, because Lillian was very generous and good at
remembering. She and Mummy were still talking in low
tones, and Dilly heard Mummy say, *well, should I
announce it?* Without waiting for a reply, Mummy said
loudly, in her speech-giving voice, *everyone. Listen, please,
everyone!* The room fell quiet again.

Mummy's expression was now the one related to
dreadful news and dismay. An almost operatic gurn. Her
brow was deeply rippled, mouth collapsing in the corners. Her hands were held to her chest. *There's been an
accident. They've found, well, a body, it seems, just very
close to us, down by the weir.* Her eyes were extremely
bright; with tears, Dilly realised. Sometimes things did
actually make Mummy very upset. There were gasps of
surprise and sympathy, and a few comments and questions, *awful, who, when, should Peter go and lend a
hand?* Mummy was drawn back into the group, *no, not
identified yet*, she was saying, expertly, though she'd
known the information only since Lillian had arrived.

Lillian set the present down on the sofa next to Dilly
and perched the other side. She had on the same trousers
that Dilly was wearing. The front pleat was perfect.
Lillian always looked so beautiful. She smiled. *Are you
all right, Dilly? Sorry about the bad news.* Dilly smiled

too and nodded, looked back at the scone on the plate. *No Sam today? No, not today.* Dilly took another bite. *Oh well, never mind. This is nice.* Lillian's voice fell a little. *I ran into your dad on the way. He said to say happy birthday. Do you think he'll pop in?* Dilly looked up to see who was left at the party. The magazine lady and Cleo were engrossed in conversation. Peter had disappeared and Dominic was holding a bottle of champagne, unsure whether to open it, while Mummy still seemed preoccupied by the trauma.

It was lovely – the wrapping on Lillian's gift, the people here who really loved her, more than Sam ever would have, the second scone, feeling like giddy déjà vu. She already knew everything, could see the body laid out on the towpath, covered by layers and layers of sodden dishevelled rags, a halo of river water leaking around it. The police had cordoned off the scene, and an ambulance was parked up on the road near the punting station. Figures in white medical suits were lifting the yellow tape, stepping underneath, and carefully approaching the lump that had been dragged out of the water. They were kneeling down and gently uncovering the body, peeling off the wet clothes, lifting the heavy wet skirt of the gown away from the face, taking off pieces of rotten fruit, and the red headband, folding back the long, furred ears, and the face underneath, so peaceful and untormented, was hers.

Who Pays?

Beyond the village, to the east, there is forest. It is very old. No one remembers its name. It has belonged to several countries, empires and tribes, and it has remained unbelonging, its own nation. Inside are the first trees of the world, whose leaves have learned broadness to collect light. The forest can be crossed in a day on foot, half a day with a steady horse or a donkey cart, faster if there are wolves. Whenever there are wars along the border, more wolves come.

In the middle of the forest, where green is richest, lies a sacred well. It sits like a funnel in the floor, sloping sides, moss-lined, with a small stepped wall on which it is possible to sit and rest and peer down the hole, where space becomes dark sound. There is no rope, no bucket with which to draw and drink. The Well of Simeon. Or the Well of Mevlâna. The oldest villagers just call it the Well of Souls. They do not come here. Whoever built it, whoever raised the spring, danced, performed reversals or miracles, no one is sure.

The walls inside are one hand-width wider than the tallest man's arm-span. Its stones are the blue of other regions, carved and carried in. Blue as buried bone. Or sea-dreamt. Or star-fallen. And its water – so clear, so cold. It might bleed from the heart of the earth.

In the spring and in the autumn, the young men of the village come. Ahmet, Selim, Sait, Nazım, Adnan, maybe with a younger eager brother, or a visiting cousin. They come with beer and salad, instruments, a bleating lamb, home-made rakı. As many as can fit in the cart, riding backwards, legs dangling. The trumpet-player, Fikret, blue-eyed and endlessly teased, plays tunes as they ride. These are good friends, childhood companions. The well celebration is an old tradition, told by grandfathers and grandmothers, forgotten for a generation but, now, lived again.

Sometimes, the young women of the village come for the first part of the evening, on borrowed horses, or on foot, single-file, taking turns to trample the grass. Eyes held for long moments, the exchange of scarves, sweet tarts and sips of beer, the freedom of twilight. This is a country between dictators, a country of momentary festivity and hope. There might be dancing. Someone might whisper a beautiful line in an ear: *The wound is the place where the light enters.* Or sweet, promissory names. *Balım, sevgilim.* All this before the tyranny of in-laws, and children, and bedroom rituals. Before the rakı the women ride home again, in darkness, carrying burning torches, scorching the low trees, leaving the young men to their longing, and their headaches.

What the women do when they come to the well alone, at other times of the year, nobody really knows. Talk of witches, body-splitters, child-removers, though their mothers walked them innocently through the woods as infants, gathering hazelnuts. On the last day of her first blood it's said a girl can smell truffle deep in the soil, blind, an intuitor of earth. One lumpy, fungal skull dug up, weighed and sold to a chef in the city, and there's a fortune for her family. She might even throw it in a sack and run, get away from goats and children, try her hand at a bar in Kadıköy, why not.

It's also said that women see things here. In the Well of Simeon, or Mevlâna, in the Well of Souls. What do they see? Futures. The only useful thing.

This spring, it begins with a coin. Ahmet, the oldest, married for two years with two children already – his wife smells so good to him, he smells so good to her, they just can't stop – has, for the last few seasons, hosted his friends before the journey to the forest. A preparatory meal is taken. How much ravioli young men eat! He and Halime are rolling and drying and stuffing and folding all week. Enough! When the boys arrive, Ahmet tells them that in one of the hundred pieces of ravioli a coin has been sealed, tucked up like a baby in a crib.

Whoever taps his tooth on it must host dinner before the next celebration. You can keep the money, he says, buy a sack of flour. Agreed? The ravioli has a touch of nutmeg, steams in the bowls, a Bulgarian grandmother's recipe. Yes, yes, sure, sure, they say, and the forks begin to move.

Halime watches them eat, her youngest baby drowsing on her breast. She seems a little sad, a little withdrawn. Perhaps the given coin has made her nervous. The men – boys, most of them – laugh and joke, eat like their wives and mothers never feed them. Would-be butcher, labourer, vintner, clerk, an almost-soldier, storyteller, and a falconer, though there's little use in birds. One blue-eyed, one so shy he cannot look her in the eye, one so calm it seems his world is reconciled. Weak and cunning souls, strong and humble. Which of them will leave the village? Who will prosper, who will fail? Who will call the fate of others? The women talk of it, when they gather for the washing, or for prayers.

Halfway through the meal – *click* – the hard edge is bitten, the coin discreetly transferred into a pocket. Once the bowls are emptied, the donkey tacked to the cart, the bottles rattled on board, the men loaded, the trumpet unsnapped from its shabby case, buffed on Fikret's sleeve and sounded, they are off. *Yarak!* Laughter. These are friends for a lifetime, they think, friends who could survive battles, even with each other.

Through the village they ride, past the church, past the mosque, past the paddocks of bearded goats. Jokes about sisters, jokes about last year's rakı – who got sick, who fell over? Fiko! But he's not allowed to stop playing the trumpet, can't speak in his own defence. Past the fire-stone where Fatma is patting dough, as she has for sixty years. She holds up her hand – three fingers, like three horns. Past the first, magnificent trees, their trunks turned and twisted like art forms, and into the ancient, green light of the forest. Lamb led behind on rope, bleating.

Adnan has the reins; he's that type, getting ready for action, military papers sitting on his father's desk. Selim is wondering if Nermin will come, how will she wear her hair, up off her shoulders or loose? Did the girls say that they were coming? Sait has a book of verse, and reads while the trumpet rests . . . *My eyes can't get enough of the trees* . . . It is respectfully appreciated. Young men are nothing if not understudy poets – imams, kings, despots, loafers, all of them. The trumpet sounds again, popular songs, almost in tune, then quietens. For the forest has its own music. It is played by the wind like a thousand reeds, by the birds with their lilts and trills. Even the momentary silence is orchestral. The donkey, dumb and obedient, trots on, takes the uphills and unevens without fuss, pauses, shits, continues.

Evening begins to smoke between the branches. The

leaves are luminescing, lit by the sun's day-long love. The men are quiet now. The lamb is quiet too, tired, given over to its destiny. Shadows seem to follow in the trees. The glimmer of an amber eye. Kurt, someone whispers. But no, the shadows do not lope like hunters, they simply melt away. Nearly there, to the Well of Simeon, or Mevlâna, the Well of Souls. Some of the women might already be waiting, with cut cucumber and mint and tomatoes, smiles. *Hope's honey*, Sait says. The beer is getting warm. The knife is blind, needs sharpening. Soon there will be a fire.

It is very green in the clearing by the well – there might be lamps of tsavorite hung between the branches. There might be spirits in the air above the void. They arrive and marvel for a moment. But time is getting on. They unload. The donkey is released, let loose in the tender grass. The men set to, preparing the ground, whittling a spit, rigging the fire and setting it alight. They put blankets down, just in case. Nazım, butcher's boy, though twenty-three, runs the knife along a steel. He steps to the side, trips the lamb, drags it struggling only a little, and sits astride. He tells Sait to hold the bowl below the neck, finds the gentle spot. *Bismillah*. A few kicks, and its head bucks back, the quick, bright river is released. A different kind of poetry, my friend, he says. The dismantlement begins – legs, shanks, ribs, liver put to float in the red bowl like a prize, indifferent head.

Not much will go to waste. The others watch, with varying degrees of keenness for suffering, then resume their occupations in the camp.

And the well waits. Waits, with its deep, invisible eye, its patience of saints, the patience of eternity. Until! The warm beer! It can be lowered and cooled to perfect temperature in that ice-cold water. Good idea, Ahmet! Today he's full of them. They load the bottles in a sack, cast about for rope like sailors in a fever. Surely there is some? No? Yes! The lamb's lead! It's dry, a bit shabby, but long enough, and good for purpose. It is wound around the sackcloth's neck and knotted, the clinking clanking load sent across the wall and down into the borehole. Down, down, it goes, and disappears into the dark. A telltale splashing echo when it meets the water. Give it half an hour, Ahmet says, it will be like drinking frost. Meanwhile, the fire's flames have lifted and settled. The first meat is skewered on the spit and roasted on the charcoal. But where are the girls? Aren't they coming?

There's talk of opening the rakı, but it is foolish talk. Not before the food, boys! Fikret plays the trumpet again, something fast to speed the cooling of the beer. Twenty minutes? Good enough, and they are thirsty. Selim and Ahmet take up the rope and begin to pull the prize. Clink, clank, go the bottles. The sack is wet and heavy, heavy as an ox! They heave. They haul. Up, up, the thing comes dripping, swaying, almost to the wall. But look, the knot at the sack's neck has slipped – none of these men know how to perform murder yet, only to imagine – and its throttle-hold softens. The rope goes slack. The men stagger back. The beer splashes down, into the well of Simeon, Mevlâna, into the Well of Souls. Can anyone see the bottles? Are they lost? Are they floating? That's a lot of beer! *Hassiktir!* Now what?

It is Adnan who volunteers, of course. He will go in and get it. Can't have their last week's wages go to waste. The others aren't so sure. The well is wide, its stones are smooth, polished by some prehistoric mason's hand, or by the sea, or rubbed imperviously by heaven – it can't be climbed. Adnan is not a spider. So lower me, then, he says, it's only water. He picks the rope, puts it around his waist, threads it through his legs and underneath his balls. Laughter. Jokes about opera, and doesn't he want children? No, I want a beer, he says, before the army dries me out.

He climbs across the wall, clings and braces. His friends take up the strain. He tests the tautness of the rope, tugs and bounces, faces the dark tunnel. *Hazırım!* Then, hand over hand, the boys release their burden, and down goes Adnan. Heavier than an ox! Jokes about ravioli, how many pieces has he eaten? One hundred? Laughter. And the gold, he calls. Gold, comes up the echo. What's that, Captain? Gold, gold! The rope sings uncertainly against the wall, its strands begin to struggle. It was me, he shouts.

Me. Me. I got the coin. The coin. The words come up from nowhere, like a confession from a dungeon. The company cheers, sending flocks of birds fluttering from the tree-tops. Hand over hand, steadily, they send their friend into the world below. The rope is running out, fraying and unravelling – get a move on, boys. He must be nearly there, about to secure the beer, a hero for the day, a legend in the making.

The borehole swims in darkness; no light inside this wound. The unreflecting surface seems to wink. And so the rope, by choice or by collusion, by chance or fate's intention, breaks. The men fall back and over, one on top of the other, scrambling to get up and calling out and calling down. Adnan! Adnan! *Tamam?* But there is only silence. Strange silence. Silence, like the spirit's longest suffering. In their dreams to come across the years, they'll never hear a plunging cry, a shout for help, not even one small ripple. It is as if that fall is endless.

And where are the women? Still no sign. They are not riding those noble horses bred from Arabians, bowing low under the heavy trees. They are not weaving through the forest, one behind the other, like wolves, taking turns to flatten down a path. They are at home. They are sitting around Halime's table, perhaps discussing their lives, their children, the children they would have or the men they might marry, the roads out of the village, the wars their grandmothers endured. The usual things.

No. Not this time. Tonight, as the moon rises above the roof of forest, they are sitting quietly, holding hands. On the table in front of them is an unopened bottle of rakı, glasses, a jug of ice water that will charm the solution milky. A coiled length of rope. Good rope, fit for any purpose, salvage, cattle, the binding of wives and daughters by an uncivil army, the hanging of those who will not change their names. Who sees? Who pays? Always the women. They have agreed. If one of them breaks hold of her sisters' hands, they will all stand, and they will go immediately, as fast as they can, into the forest, as if late for a party or an accidental rescue. It is hard. One of them is his cousin. They played together when she and he were small; she thought that it was play. How can the weight of one man go on to break a country? How can knowing be unseeing, or visions free to ruin? Their grip is tight. Their knuckles white and risen. Fatma, half-handed daughter of the last violence, says to them, do not, do not ask to be forgiven.

In the Well of Souls, the water is so cold that it can shatter bones; it can sting the brain and seize the heart within a minute. It is so clear that it can strip the body of all reason, rob the mind of all possession and ambition, stop those who are, as if they never were, so they will never be. Extraordinary, intolerable, uncorrupted water. Water, born from the middle of the earth, that pure and secret place no sun or human hand has ever warmed. Water, come from the past, in one form or another, rain, river, sea, thoughts like tears in clouds, as old as it is new, designed to serve no purpose other than its future.

Orton

It had taken three buses to get to the village and she was very tired. She was tired all the time, tired in the mornings as if she'd worked a whole day, and breathless at night. This journey was the longest she'd made all year. One bus to Kendal, one to Shap Junction, and then, finally, the last, over the moors to Orton. There had been a lot of waiting between connections, watching teenagers rattle coins into vending machines and paw chocolate bars out of the flaps. The buses were all old, with steep steps. On the last, the driver had risen from his seat to help her up, nice man. She hadn't any bags, just her favourite purse, and so she told him she could manage, and she did manage, just.

She sat near the front, watching the yellow grassland flush past, the brinjal and sorrel hills beyond. Lumpy cloud. Emptiness. Travelling back up the county this way had been strangely moving, like watching a history of her life playing. She'd come less and less over the years. Gatherings, funerals – lots of people she'd known were gone, even her younger brother. The motorway spooled over a bridge above the moorland. Dark ponies with ragged manes cropped the turf, and a few sheep stumbled on to the road without attempting to cross. The bus trilled over a series of shiny new cattle grids. The stuffy air, growling engine and petrol waft reminded her of those provincial school buses she'd taken. Hard, vibrating seats that the older girls said could give you an orgasm if you sat right, legs open. *Go on, Sharon, give it a go.* Sometimes one of them shrieked loudly and the others would laugh. She looked down at her legs, very slender under the silk frock. She inched them apart.

In her purse she had the mobile phone Mia insisted she keep, fully charged, a bit of cash, the code to her setter and its little black remote. Dr Ong had given her these items after the operation, with a folder of information about how everything worked and possible side effects of the surgery – there weren't any, it turned out, other than a tiny scar below one breast, and the peculiar knowledge that she was no longer an automatic being. There was lots of paperwork to sign, pages and pages of it, legal documents too. That had been more tiring than the anaesthetic.

The implant was half the size of her little fingernail – extraordinary considering the job it did. She'd been told to memorise the code, like a bank number, then destroy the hard copy. She hadn't, of course; she was never any good at remembering numbers. They'd given her echo pictures of her heart too – before and after. She couldn't tell the difference.

Shall I frame them? she'd asked Dr Ong.

A slight smile from the tidy, suited woman who had been the one to part her ribs and position the thing, and whose consulting room was full of old-fashioned medical diagrams of the organ, its open valves and chambers.

If you have any questions, come back and see me, the doctor had told her. Do you understand everything, Mrs Lydford?

Yes.

You understand your options?

Yes.

A controlled environment is best for any reprogramming that you may wish to consider.

Yes.

She did understand. The off switch was hers. *Non-compulsory intima assistance* was the official term for this new generation of devices, for those with terminal failure. *Enders*, as she'd joked to her husband. *I'm an ender, Kenneth.* She hadn't voted for the current government, they'd always seemed a bit middle-ish and over-clever, but they'd got the health service back up out of its throes, and this new legislation was fine by her. How could you not own yourself, anyway? Who else would, some hound-master God? Anyway, she didn't have to worry about that. All she had to do was ring in to a call centre and answer several questions, to make sure she wasn't loopy, then proceed. It did seem simple enough to be dangerous, she supposed.

She'd thought about wearing a hat for the journey, but it seemed too formal, a bit overdone. The blue silk dress was her favourite, though, and the long woollen coat – good choices. There were no photographs in her purse. She'd taken them all out before leaving home. Too difficult having all their faces along with her, making her sentimental. She'd tidied, paid the bills, turned the water off, made sure the neighbour would feed Poss. That was enough.

The moor hadn't changed. The grass was restless, bleached and occasionally bright auburn when the sun lit it. Long walls ran upwards towards the fells, and the cleaved limestone pavements sat pale and dull on the slopes. Wind-leant trees, peat gullies, flocks of heather and the occasional darting thing. Under the clouds, great dark shadows moved across the hills. Nothing extraordinary, but still beautiful, she thought.

The bus took the corners fast; the driver knew the exact speed and tilt he could get away with. There were only three other passengers, all dressed in walking gear, rucksacks propped like neon turtles on the seats behind them. She closed her eyes, and when she opened them there was the village. A cluster of stone gables, grey as the crayfish, streams running off the main channel, and the stout white church tower. Fifty-four years was how long it'd been since she'd seen Orton. And him. He was dead now too, she knew that. A friend she still corresponded with in Penrith had told her – some kind of male cancer. Maybe the same thing Kenneth had died of. What was it about men that they didn't ring the doctor when they couldn't piss straight? Ken would have been hurt to know she'd chosen to come here, instead of staying at home. Poor Ken. But the marriage had been mostly happy, a few years of low-grade depression and arguing after the baby, normal tensions really, but good on the whole, even if it was not what she'd expected. They'd felt comfortable with each other, which was what counted in the end, probably. He'd been a nice lover; he got very hot when they made love, dripped sweat on her. He didn't take it personally if she couldn't finish. They'd done it into their sixties – a lot of their friends hadn't. When they'd handed him Mia, while they were stitching her, he'd cried and said, *Oh my little one, oh poppet.* He'd never forgotten birthdays. And he'd been there, kneeling on the kitchen floor with her, when the first palpitations hit. How could Orton match all that? he'd have asked her.

But Ken was gone. Mia was in South Africa and seemed settled. She was tired.

A controlled environment, Dr Ong had said. That had made her smile. She'd pictured a white room, some stemless orchids, a hovering clock. She'd thought of her mother hanging laundry in the barn. And then she'd pictured the moors. Churned tracks, the riot of moss and tan, and a great, belting wind off the Pennines. There was pain in her back, her hips, her feet, she was so bloody bored of it. And a feeling had arrived she couldn't quite explain, of nothingness underfoot, like crossing the river, hovering between stepping stones.

The bus stopped outside the village shop. Bistro-style tables and chairs were set up on the pavement. The walkers disembarked, heaving their bags on to their backs. She pulled herself up and made her way down the steps and this time she didn't prevent the driver holding her arm. The door shushed closed and the bus pulled away. There it was, that smell. Residents of coastal towns always talked about it – ions, salt and weed rot, the signature of the sea. She lived only a few miles away from the bay now, in the mild south of the county. Ken's home, really. But moorland was different. It was not clean or simple, not a high note. All that bog and bark, the game of animals and wet feathers, flowers scented like discharge, mineral rain, and a cold black peaty sweat. It was like the smell of sex, the smell after sex, of everything combined and complicated and dying back. She couldn't really separate it from him.

Funny what stuck. He wasn't even her boyfriend; she'd just met him for the day, on a sort of date one Saturday. He'd been looking at her across the bandstand in town most of one week. Then he'd asked her out. He'd picked her up in his dad's car, and brought her for a walk. Orton was the village between their villages. He was quiet for one of the Grammar boys; they were usually confident and larky, would go for your neck and leave a sucked welt, or burrow a hand down the back of your pants; they always tried to get things going. But this one was all put away and concentrated, not a talker or a hand-holder. They'd walked quite a long way over the moors on the sheep tracks; it was fairly awkward, she'd thought. At one point he'd pointed to a blackened area of burnt gorse and told her he'd set it alight. Just him, not his brother, he said. As if that mattered somehow. She'd had on plimsoles and a long chiffon skirt, a little vest and lilac lacy bra; her arms were bare. The ground-water had soaked her feet and stained the canvas of her shoes. It was May, hot in shelters, but the wind was cold on her skin, it still had winter's sere. At the limestone pavement he'd stopped.

I think we should go here.

I have to get back soon.

Not yet.

They'd sat on the uneven stools of rock, backs to the fells, not even facing each other. It felt like a disaster, being stranded miles out with this spare part. All she was planning was how to get home without having to get a lift from him. Finding a phone box, reversing the charges, getting someone to fetch her. But then he'd turned and put his hand on her leg. Before even kissing her he'd brushed aside her skirt like cobwebs and had begun to stroke her, very softly, as if he were stroking a breakable and delicate thing, a baby rabbit. She'd caught her breath. It was the first time someone else doing it had felt right, not clumsy, not uncomfortable. He'd knelt down in front, looking up.

Do you want me to?

Do I want you to what?

Lick you out.

He was shockingly unembarrassed. There was a look of remedial honesty on his face. It was simply a question, an option, no guile to it. He was still stroking her.

Can you stop if I ask you to?

He took off her wet, dirty shoes, one by one – the only romantic act. Her underwear he pulled to the side, and after he'd begun, when it was clear she wasn't going to stop him, he'd stripped her pants off over her legs and thrown them into the grass. She looked to the side, at the patches of bright moss in the stones. Some of it she didn't like, when his tongue went stiff and sharp, but he knew, he could hear that, and he repeated whatever had made her sounds soften or get louder. He knew what he was doing; maybe he'd been taught; she didn't want to think by who. The older girls were always talking about which ones were *naturals*, which ones bit too much or came too soon or liked it if a girl was on top. After a while it was unbearable, and she'd pushed his head away.

What do you want me to do?

Now she was just tired. She didn't want to walk far, she couldn't, just past the cottages and on to the howe, so she could feel that upland wind flowing off the grass and bracken. She took the phone out of her bag and checked for a signal. It was low, but registered. There would be a few minutes from the call to authorisation, she knew. She wondered what they would say to her, if anything. *Good luck, Mrs Lydford. God bless you* – she hoped not that. She'd written to Mia, a proper letter, not an email, that would arrive too late in the post, but would explain, as best she could. They'd had a short decent phone call the day before. Perhaps Mia wouldn't understand, perhaps she would; her daughter often surprised her. In truth, Mia didn't need her, and that was how it should be.

She went into the shop. There was a magazine rack, sweets, crisps and shelves of beans and pasta, a fridge of local meats and a little table with pottery for sale. Things had come back around to local crafts and produce. She was glad about that. Her parents had given up farming after the supermarkets arrived and the subsidies were cut, then had run the place as a B&B, the big barns empty, pots of flowers outside the front door. Not many had adapted that well. A neighbour in the valley had hanged himself in his shed. On hearing the news, her father had nodded. *Carl had his ideas. I respect that.*

She hadn't understood. Now she was older than her mother had been. Her mum had had a bad heart too. Blue hands and feet and the tip of her nose in winter. With her, it had been quicker. She'd dropped like a sack-load of rusk in the courtyard and the ambulance had stalled coming across the river ford. She felt a bit of lovely pain, remembering. It never went away altogether, that kind of loss, but sat about you like weather, chang-ing, getting up a gale from time to time. And for the others. Her brother. Kenneth. She was sorry he was dead too; sorry she hadn't known him later in life. What kind of man would he have been? She often wondered. But there were those who could only fit into the past, couldn't come onwards with the turn of the years. A love might never be at all, if there wasn't symmetry, a moment to try it. She'd thought a lot about the heart, all its functions and associations. Dr Ong's hearts were so simple-looking – blue and red pockets, a few holes, a few tubes.

The girl behind the shop counter was about eighteen. She wore a fleece, trim jeans, no make-up. Her skin was totally under control. She didn't look worldly – maybe that was the point these days. To be it, but not look it, or to have an online persona that was your opposite, that saved you the job but made you feel false and inferior. Was she going up on to the moor? Was she clear about her yeses and noes? Girls now were supposed to be more adventurous, weren't they, and angry, and they had their own cars and jobs and phones. Were they getting lessons in how to know yourself early? She doubted it; they all looked so sad and thin.

She bought a packet of Orton beef. It was expensive, useless, and would sit inside her purse getting warm, but so what.

Could I have a tea to go? she asked the girl.

Earl Grey or normal or herbal?

She pointed to the English Breakfast. She'd never liked the fennelly or camomile ones Mia preferred; they all tasted like hay.

Don't forget to save, she said to the girl, who looked confused.

The hot-water pipe hissed. She took the tea in its paper cup outside and sat on one of the wrought-iron chairs. The sky was still lumpy, greyish. March. Soon the evenings would be getting longer, blossoms unfurling on the hazels and the hawthorns. The walkers from the bus were consulting a plastic map, gazing up at the Pennines.

She sipped the tea. She took the phone, the setter remote and the piece of paper with the code out of her purse, and she called the number. She was afraid, of course. She might change her mind. She'd asked Dr Ong at the last cardiology clinic how it might be, how it might feel. Would it be painful? It was all right if so, she thought, she'd known pain. But would her heart struggle on, try to reinstate itself? She didn't want to end up in between. It made her think of cattle that the bolt-gun had mishit in the line.

Not painful, we don't think, the doctor had said. Your heart is no longer capable of autonomy, so we would expect swift discontinuance of the organ, and across the whole body.

The doctor had spoken quietly. They were perhaps not supposed to discuss such things speculatively. There was supposed to be a plan. They went through the usual tests; she watched the ultrasound picture of the muscles shuddering and contracting, on cue. Then, as she was leaving, Dr Ong had said something odd.

It is perhaps beautiful and powerful.

That slight, enigmatic medical smile.

Like a climax, of sorts.

She didn't have to wait in a call queue. The voice was pleasant, intelligent, a young man from Newcastle. He asked her the questions, her memorable information, the name of the prime minister, and she answered correctly.

I didn't vote for him, she said, and the man laughed politely.

Your passcode is active, he said, is there anything else I can help you with today?

Did he understand what his job really was, she wondered. She thanked him and said no and hung up. She took another sip of tea. One or two spots of rain could be felt. The remote vibrated on the table. She unlocked it, typed in the numbers carefully, pressed enter, and set it back down. Her hand was shaking a little. There was a short beep. Borrowed days, she thought, all of them.

Not far away, there was a bench near the steep pack-horse bridge, where the common opened out on to fellside. The river there was fast and shallow. She remembered the spot, flies above the water and the pale mouths of trout coming up and kissing the surface. She'd sat there afterwards with him and watched the water for a while, watched him upending rocks in the current looking for crayfish, feeling stunned, but unafraid. She'd never felt so unafraid in her life, even with the stinging trickle between her legs.

What about you? she'd said.

She hadn't really understood the preferences of men. She'd pulled his face to hers, his glistening mouth, because it seemed wrong not to. He broke away and continued. She hadn't known him, or liked him as she had some of the others, but it didn't matter to her body.

When she came it was like a blind goldness, like staring at the sun, so that she was gone, she was its soft destroyed atoms. That brilliant bursting sensation all through and up and into her, and she couldn't breathe, couldn't control any part of what made and drove her. She heard the clink of his belt coming undone, and he was inside. With the others there had been a few moments of bareness, before stopping, anxiety for days after about the risk, the before-rain drizzle. It was as if he, and she, knew the purpose of it all, and there had never been anything as honest or as free as that commitment, not in all the years of love and the practices of marriage, the planning of children, the bonds favoured by people.

Both of them unable to stop, as if dragged into a beautiful slaughtering machine. Even after he'd come he didn't still, but kept moving. Then he finally lay against her, shivering, while she looked away. Carrion bones and a ring of stripped tawny fur nearby, the smell of burnt wood, and the black return of everything to peat. Afterwards, they'd walked back down the sheep tracks, as silently as they'd come up, and gone to the river, then gone home, and not ever spoken again, not even looked at each other across the street in town. Another life started, which was the proper one, the one that comes after a sacrifice.

She stood up, took off her coat, left it on the chair for someone to find and maybe keep, and began to walk. The bridge and the bench were not far. She would get there. She would settle herself, arrange the skirts of her dress and wait. It would not be bad for whoever found her. It was nature; no, it was what nature would have done, a while ago, were it not for the brilliance of human invention. And no, she wasn't afraid, here in Orton. She hadn't been afraid that day, over half a century ago – that's what she would have explained to everyone, if she could. And he hadn't been afraid either, when there was usually so much fear in life and of life, all those named and nameless fears that finally exhausted and controlled everything, when really there was no control, not in the end.

Sudden Traveller

You breastfeed the baby in the car, while your father and brother work in the cemetery. They are clearing the drains of leaves and silt, so your mother can be buried. November storms have brought more rain than the valley has ever seen. The iron gates of the graveyard are half gone, the residents of the lower-lying graves are swimming. Water trickles under the car's wheels. The river has become a lake; it has breached the banks, spanned the valley's sides. And still the uplands weep. On the radio they have been talking about rescue squads, helicopters, emergency centres in sports parks and village halls. The army is bringing sand. They have been comparing measurements from the past one hundred years. The surface of the floodwater is decorated with thousands of rings as the rain comes down.

Inside the car is absolute stillness. When he is finished, the baby sleeps against your side. There are only two small feeds a day now. His mouth has become a perfect tool and you no longer have any marked sensation, no tingling, no pressure across the chest wall as the milk lets down. His mouth remains slightly open, his cheeks flushed. There are bright veins in his eyelids, like light filaments in leaves. He rests heavily against you, hot, breathing softly, like a small machine, an extra organ worn outside the body. You could try to place him carefully on the front seat, under a blanket, get out and help clear the leaves. You would like to feel the cold air against your face and hands as it streams over the mountains. You would like to work with the men. But you dare not move.

You sit in the car, watching reefs of cloud blow across the valley, watching the trees bow and lean and let go of their last leaves, hearing the occasional lost call between your father and brother, and feeling the infant heat against your side. Nobody warned you about this part – suspension from the world. Waiting to rejoin. The baby is some kind of axis, a fixed point in time, though he grows every day, fingers lengthening, face passing through echoes of all your relatives, and the other relatives, heart chambers expanding, blood reproducing. It is like holding a star in your arms. All the moments of your life, all its meanings and dimensions, seem to lead to and from him.

In the hospital, he played with the plastic bracelet the nurse gave him, identical to the one your mother was wearing. He threw it on the floor and everyone, even the consultant, picked it up and gave it back, laughing. No one could resist such a game. Joy in the midst of trauma; such a welcome relief. *Should we write his name on it*, a nurse asked. *No, no*, you said. *Absolutely not.* Then again, you kept the tiny one from his birth in a box of medical mementos – the woollen hat they put on him, despite the heat of July, despite his raw scalp, the subterranean surgical thread they'd used to stitch you closed, its two blue beads. The power of artefacts, like a ritualistic hoard. Occult. Perhaps, in keeping such items, you have created a dark charge.

Good as gold, the nurses said as he played on the ward floor. He smiled at the ladies in their beds, ladies of ruin, gowned, chronically pained, with systems in shutdown, embarrassed by their smells. You could see his effect, like tonic, for them. *What a poppet*, they said. *Bonnie lad, you've come to see your Granmammy.* He watched your mother jerk under the white sheet, too young, of course, to understand. It might have seemed like a silly game. You took him outside when the nurses changed her pads, knowing, knowing she would want that privacy, and walked him on your feet down the corridor, holding his wrists, his operator, his avatar. You bought coffee for everyone in the hospital cafe – your dad, brother, even your niece and nephew – then came back to take your place at the vigil.

The nurses were talking about death around her bed, casually, the normalness of dying, and at first you were horrified, you wanted to tell them to stop, shut up, it would frighten your mother to hear such things. Then you began to see they were, in fact, comforting her, better than you could. Dying: like having a wash, like stirring sugar into tea, or laying out cutlery. It was the first instruction of what would become a vital list of instructions, bringing the experience close, feeling its cool brush against your skin.

You sat your son on your mother's bed, keeping him away from the intravenous pump pushing morphine. Enough morphine to relieve, but not to render insensate, yet – let her be conscious for the goodbyes. They had removed the feeding tubes, which was also an act of kindness, no matter how counter-intuitive. The baby reached for the dish and the sponge with which you had been wetting her dry mouth. He reached for your mother's twitching fingers. Everything in her was breaking down. They told you some part of her would know what was going on in the room around her, she would be able to hear at least and at last, and yes, you think she did know. Your son's name was the only word she could say properly, though she was trying and trying to talk, her voice hoarse, making no sense. When you held him close, and put her hand on his head, on that beautiful drift of hair above his neck, her

eyes focused for a moment, on you, on him. She said,
Hello –

The ward was full. The hospital was full. Winter, the
season of infection, of brutalisation of the weak and the
old. Within half a day, the nurses had found her –
through some complicated political subterfuge – a private
room. Less than forty-eight hours, the consultant had
said, once they'd admitted her and run tests. You forget
exactly who broke that piece of news – your dad, your
brother, one of the doctors, maybe. You were already en
route to the hospital, halfway up the motorway, on
speakerphone. The night before, she'd fallen out of bed,
and your father and the neighbour could not lift her
back in, though she weighed, by then, very little. You
knew it was not good. You had been keeping, in fact, a
small overnight bag under your bed, ready to go. Like
the weeks when your son was due. *Thank you*, you said,
to whichever green-winged angel told you, *thanks for
letting me know.* You did not pull over into a lay-by or
service station, though you were advised to sit quietly for
half an hour, to have a cup of strong tea, maybe call
someone to comfort you. Who idles after such news?
Instead, you gripped the steering wheel, accelerated up
to ninety and switched the wipers on. The baby slept in
his tilted seat. There were already weather warnings,
talk of road closures, diversions. There were clouds the
colour of iron ahead of you.

Now you are sitting quietly, parked in the little pull-off beside the village cemetery, with water surrounding the car, in twilight-hour light, though it is eleven fifteen in the morning. It has been eleven fifteen for much longer than a minute, you are sure. The clock does not move. The baby burns against your ribs, emitting, absorbing. Now there is time to sit, all the time in the world, but no more time for her, or him, or you. Time: the most unrelatable concept. If you stepped off this planet, you'd need no such identifier; everything would bend and fold, repeat, or just release. You'd have no age. You'd cease to be definite. What would that mean? Many selves, all in existence? Before- and afterlives? Some kind of scientific proposition you don't quite understand. The truth is, where you are now, caught inside the storm, lost inside its eye, so tired, so undefined, you could be these other yous, inhabited, replaced.

Your brother carries a bag of wet leaves out of the cemetery. His coat is stained, his trousers soaked to the thigh. He looks towards the car, doesn't smile. He and his wife and their kids are staying at your parents' house too. Your father's house. The house where you were raised. All of you, over the last week, have been driving to and from the hospital, dozing in the chairs, bringing supplies. Only your father remained in full attendance, requesting clothes, his medicines, her favourite Christmas tree decoration. The nurses were kind about suspending the restrictions, you must remember to write, thank them, do something, send them a set of tea-cups, perhaps; they drink so much tea.

Tell me when, your brother had said to your dad the last night at the hospital, as he was leaving, *tell me to come and I'll get there in time*. The hospital is nearly an hour's drive away in the day, slow country roads, then steep northern motorway. Not exactly a swift journey. But at night the north has other dimensions. Empty roads shine like dark wounds through the mountains. Everything warps. You almost believe he would have got there. Four a.m. was when her breathing finally changed, but your brother was so worn out he didn't hear the phone ringing. Didn't pick up the message, your father's anguished plea: *Come now*. A neighbour knocking on the door broke the news in the morning, and then your brother went out on the moor with the dogs and nobody knows what came next, but the dogs made their own way home. He will not forgive himself, you can see it in the way his body moves between the graves. Penance. Hard labour. He wanted so badly to be there in that final moment.

You did not want to be there. You were afraid of that last inhalation, its lack of echo. You did not want to see the door close. You wanted those dry, wood-tongued breaths to go on and on, selfishly, fearfully, even though, when you had the room to yourself, you told her it was

OK to go, you told her you and the others would be OK. *Just sleep, Mum.*

But you did go to the morgue. You stood and you looked. She was so altered she seemed like another substance, not flesh. She looked like an image in the only dream you would ever have thereafter. Why did you go? You've asked yourself. Because you had to see, be sure. Your brother did not come into that back room. He sat with your niece and nephew and drank exceptionally well-made coffee with the morticians, allowed them to steward him, even to humour him, so good were they at their service, those two placid, blue-robed gladiators – you must write to them too. Your brother's wife came in with you. *I don't think I can touch her,* you said, and you handed over a pair of little socks belonging to your son, and your brother's wife gently tucked them into your mum's hand, she who never considered herself brave, who exemplified, in that moment, all concept of courage.

Your brother dumps the bag and goes back into the cemetery. You watch him through the bars of the gates. He rakes the leaves. He kicks at the blockages with his heel. He sweeps water down the culverts. He would climb into the sky if he could and hammer shut the clouds, command the rain to stop like some demented prophet. You could go to him and say: *She wouldn't have wanted us there. She spent her whole life making sure we would be spared such things.* After the funeral, you will say it to him.

The baby sleeps. This is his commitment. You have not really slept for several days. The undertakers – who, like the morticians, move through the darkest realms with a kind of grace and levity you can't fathom – have told you this is usual for the bereaved. Too much adrenalin has been dispensed into the body. Unusual psychological events need to be processed. All that survivalist caffeine has stoked you up too high. You are so tired there are moments you are not sure if you are awake any more. It feels like those early newborn days, the fugue state of new motherhood, when the baby was in a separate plastic cot at your bedside. There was no involution yet, they couldn't stop the bleeding and chemicals were being used to shrink your womb. There was talk of a transfusion. You couldn't stand up to lift him, so from time to time he was being handed to you, then put back in the cot. There was no milk. The trauma of surgery had arrested it, or your body wasn't ready. They were giving him formula to keep the weight on. His fontanel looked depressed. A wasp had come into the room and kept landing near his feet. Your eyes would simply not close. On the third night, you finally did sleep, and fell into a terrible kinetic dream in which your atoms were blown apart and your essence was drawn with tremendous force outwards and outwards, into the hospital room, into the sky, into black space and whatever lies at the furthest reaches, emptiness. After you'd come round, crying, hitting the alarm on the bed, you interpreted it in only one way. Transposition. The baby had come, and you would go, the universe was telling you. It was the most scared you've ever felt.

Two months later, the diagnosis came. Your mother had had backache for a while, since before you gave birth. She couldn't hold the baby either, though she tried several times and had to put him down. She was booked in for X-rays, then MRIs. You were visiting your parents at the time. They arrived home from the consultation and you saw their faces and knew what was coming. On the scans were shadows in the lungs and spine. The liver. Glands. Not yet the brain. Smoker. Decades of smoke.

It was early autumn, gilded, the gorse was going wild, so fragrant it was like another country, those long shadows running up and down the fells, quartering the fields, warm enough to swim in the river if you'd been the child you once were, river-child, bright in the evening when you walked the lanes, the baby in the sling in front of you, your abdomen still aching from the section. With therapy, there would be a year, a little more, a little less, the statistics showed. It was a very standard, very predictable cancer. Everyone should prepare, though how to prepare can never be clear. *Ask ques-*

tions, friends said. *Spend time. Take videos. Listen to stories.* Stories. There was, of course, the ongoing joy of the baby for your mother, a child whose memories would not be able to form in time to remember her.

When he is older, you will ask him: *Is there anything you remember of her? Any texture? Any sound? Smell?* You were a little older than your son's age when your mother lost her father. Too young to really know him. So it goes. People as fundamental as the sky, gone before they can be shared by future generations. You remember a little, your grandfather's arms, the faded Navy tattoos, shreds of tobacco on the tabletop and the little machine he used to roll cigarettes, him stirring a pan of cocoa. From so little, can a person be summoned? You remember London, where he lived with your nan. London one winter in the seventies while you were visiting, under all that snow, a buried city, alleys of ice, cars gone missing, frozen taps. Ever since, London has seemed in your imagination a broken winter city. You have conflated these memories, of course. Your consciousness wasn't formed, you can't have made them yourself. You have often wondered about memories that are not your own, memories of what you've been told, implanted, hereditary, even genetic. Your grandfather was a boy soldier at the Somme, one of so few who survived. He spent four decades at sea. HOLD FAST was inked on his knuckles.

In your mind, it's easy to see those words, faded, bled through the skin. Yellow gas. Drenched wool. Wounds in his legs that would swallow the shrapnel and keep it as a heavy souvenir. Those green, incalculable waves, south of the equator. But then, you've read all this, seen films, heard family stories. Your cells, your neurons, your imagination have all been manipulated.

As your son sleeps, you whisper things about your mother and your mother's history to him. You think of her. *She loved butter. She always sneezed three times. Her perfume rose a few notes above her skin. She hid much of her identity. Her grandparents crossed the border in a farm wagon to get out of their country. The rest, the unnumbered, were never spoken about. The great stirred cauldron of Europe, where so many were and are repelled, sent into exile, east and west, again and again.* What order of gifts are you trying to give him?

But here, now, in the calm warmth of the car, holding the child, a hurricane surrounding the county and shutting everything down, you can feel the river of what has passed and what is coming. The morning sky is dark. Birds are being blown between branches, forming shapes, auguring. This rain is not helping: savage, unrelenting, incanting, strange even for here, making it hard to see anything clearly or think clearly. What you sense is mutability, the selves within the self. The terror of being taken, ahead, into sheer darkness. What is coming? Not just this lesson of a dying mother. But travel into— You can do no more than intuit. You suspect your dreams are communicating far more destruction than you have interpreted, and in this you are correct. The future is a window that cannot be opened until it is opened.

Your mother's coffin is white. Lightweight. It is made of wool, from this district of wool. It is waiting quietly for her at the undertaker's, and will be covered with the flowers she loved most. Six of you will bear it from the car into the church, then to the cemetery – you and your closest cousin at the front; your tall, quiet, fourteen-year-old nephew at the back; your brother, father, and one other, who is already turning away from you and will remain faceless. Your cousin has farmed sheep for years, hefting animals on to her shoulders, bringing them into the sheds in winter gales, for lambing, or in sickness. It is one of the hardest occupations. Though she worries she is not capable, you know she is. You are worrying too, about this duty. Will you remain upright, sure-footed? Will you break down under grief? And, yes, who, after this is done, as it must be done, tomorrow, or the next day, whenever the rain permits, who will carry you?

This, you can't be told. Stories are the currency of past lives. Families, lovers, enemies, friends. You do not understand yet, who you will lose, who you will become, who will arrive. We are, all of us, sudden travellers in the world, blind, passing each other, reaching out, missing, sometimes taking hold. But, sooner than you think, after this flood, after the darkness, the loss, the loneliness, someone is going to take your hand and tell a story about the death of his grandfather. It is a story about displacement, about expulsion from a homeland, again, always, thousands fleeing for the border, making a new home. It is a story about snow as well, snow in the suburbs of a city you have not yet seen, but will see, vast, continental, where, in the year of the grandfather's death, water flooded the basement walls and froze to ice, the ground was so hard, so locked, the family worried no grave could be dug, though dug it was. The men carried the coffin, from home to mosque, traditional pall-bearers where no such occupation exists, rotating positions, bringing in new arms every so often to renew their strength. He carried it too, this teller, this future traveller. The story will feel so familiar to you. You will begin to understand that those who suffer, suffer the same. In this condition, we are never alone. The heaviness that you are going to feel when that white box is upon your shoulder, and even after it is set down, lowered, buried, and for years to follow, will, for the first time, become less. But not yet.

First, these floods, the waterlogged cemetery, people toiling to get this ruined English patch clear and open and ready to receive. Bags of muck and silt dumped at the gates. Promissory clouds in the west. The undertakers will be arriving in a while to assess the situation, to see whether the small yellow digger will be able to get in and do its work. He is young, the head of the funeral home – forty perhaps, Irish, unfazed by rain's catastrophe, by any catastrophe. You have fallen, after only a day or two in his company, in love with him, and will love him for the duration of this event. His immaculate suit. Hands with the high veins of one used to ferrying awkward human loads. He purveys the calm and rightness of what must happen at life's end. Astonishing, you think, the care with which a stranger might be tended by strangers. *Don't panic*, he says, *just don't panic.* This is his standard catchphrase, panic being, you realise, one of death's main ingredients. *Ring me*, he says, *day or night, if you want to come and see her. She is your mother. She is yours.* Your father has visited, kept her body company, brought her a letter from you with cuttings of hair from you and your son, brought her some sloe gin; it's brewing season. She is still his wife.

But she is no longer your mother. Atoms, dreams, gods, whatever the new state, she is gone. That is what you wanted to see in the mortuary. You wanted to see that she had been taken, that she was vacant. And she was, like a bad photograph of herself that failed to capture any soul, or any real likeness. Her body, which was your shared pre-language, which is the language your son speaks with you now, was empty, altered, altering, chemicals notwithstanding. Matter can't last its separation from energy. To say you could not touch her isn't true. You touched her hair, very gently, a coward, knowing this would be the least cold part, while your brother's wife did the rest. And that was the last time you saw her. That was when you gave her up.

The baby stirs, constructs a new nested position under your arm. If he were to open his eyes you could compare their colour to hers, which is very similar. Even now you know that will be a consolation over the coming years. You will say it readily to people. *They have the same blue . . . like denim.* It has occurred to you that you have been neither a very good mother nor a very good daughter over the past year. Caught between two extreme experiences, incoming and outgoing, to put it bluntly, you felt some kind of internal paralysis. People have been kind, mostly. *It's an impossible situation,* they've said, *all you can do is cope, look after your child, tell your mother you love her.* Of course, there are expectations, unspoken, and judgements. You are a woman, after all. But you have fed and dressed and cleaned the baby. You have arranged his immunisations, taken him to the swimming pool, read and sung to him. You've kept up with the antenatal group – there's a lot

of tea and cake involved, chat about managerial blow
jobs, wilted breasts for the ones who are no longer nurs-
ing, even talk of second babies, *may as well get it all
over and done with . . .* You have called and visited your
mother, helped her up the stairs and into the car for
appointments, told her the wig looks great – *really
natural* – and in fact it did, mashed her food, helped her
to the commode, cleaned up, done as much as you could.
You have operated in the capacities you've had to. But
you can't say that you felt truly present, or receptive, or
mindful. Where were you? There, but not there. Waiting
for something to change.

Now, you must wait out the rain, see what the earth
will allow. Ceremonies can happen any time, words, the
songs of grief, celebrations – these things are fine and
lost like smoke. It is the last deep ritual of commitment
that humans battle to make. The relinquishment, to fire
or soil or salt. You can see the stress on your father's and
brother's faces. They know they are fighting not just
with elements, the earth, the bloody ridiculous weather,
but with their own mortal machinery. Their voices are
becoming more and more anxious. *When is it going to
give up? Pass me that shovel. Do you think the water's
going down in the corner?* Your brother tries to check
the weather app on his phone, but, surrounded by hills
and clouds, there is no signal. As a hundred years ago,
the sky is the only way to predict. And in the west –

more anvil clouds, thick, the forge of the storm. Your brother is squatting by the drain; his elbows are dripping. Your father stands looking at the trickling slope on which is her plot, and his too. His head is bent. He might be weeping. He might be praying or thinking nothing. In this graveyard lie the bones of his own father, who died long ago, whom you never knew at all. You could place the baby on the seat of the car and go to them. But you don't.

Wait. That is all you have to do. It is a lesson from your childhood in this place. Nothing is unchanging. Rain that seems unstoppable, that seems impossible to see through, that keeps coming down, obscuring the world, washing away time, will end. Like everything else, it is only passing spirit.

And then you know how it will be. Breaking cloud, sky with discernible colour, fantastic-seeming sunlight. The rain will lift. The river will recede. Your father and brother will have dragged enough branches and mess clear of the drains for the flood to disperse. The little yellow digger will chug down the road, bow wave before it, churned wake following, and it will toil over the uneven ground to the place your father is standing now. It will set its bucket down, ready to bring up mud and roots and slop. The gravedigger, a man in his seventies who calls himself 'Fosser', after his Roman predecessors, will do something he has not done for years, possibly since he was an apprentice: he will build temporary wooden struts to keep the sodden walls of the grave from falling. And, listen, if you really need a sign, now, that something better is coming, that you will survive, that you will one day travel through kinder times, here it is. When Fosser arrives, he will climb out of the cab and he will stand looking out at the valley's expanse of water for a moment; he will come over to the car and knock on the window, which you will put down, and he will say one word to you: *Bosphorus*. Later, you will remember this. You will remember it while standing on board a ship, holding the rail, rain hammering the surface of the strait, domes and minarets and towers rising out of the mist, calls of gulls, and a man's face turned towards you, his heat against your chest as you make the crossing, not really from west to east, or east to west, but from suffering to happiness. Coincidence? Fate? Just Fosser, mentioning his last holiday, perhaps. These labourers of the other realms, of portals, these keepers of the beyond – can they predict, can they see what you cannot?

Tomorrow. Tomorrow, the hearse will swim through the remaining tides and lumber gracefully up the unmade lane to the house, looking like a black swan. Freesias will line its polished wooden shelf. Inside, the white wool coffin will cosset your mother. You will put on a long black coat and red gloves, boots. Your oldest school friend will come and mind the baby – the first day of him being fully weaned, though you had not planned it this way. The church will only be half-full, not because your mother wasn't loved, but because the roads and railways right up the western half of the country are shut. Chaos for the mourners, chaos for commuters, for everyone, homes abandoned, bridges washed away, power out. You will stand up and speak at the service, as will your father and brother, you will all manage to get through it, and your niece, only twelve years old, will read a poem about hearts within hearts, flawlessly, and she will seem so much older. Your shoulder, the shoulder upon which you usually set the baby after feeding, the shoulder where the strap of your bag hangs every day, and where there will be, in a year or two, as a protective talisman, or instructions for living, a small blue tattoo with the words *Vive ut Vivas*, your shoulder will bear one-sixth of the weight of the coffin, of the reduced, insubstantial body of your mother. The churchgoers will process through the village behind the hearse, as is tradition here, to the cemetery, where the gates will be open, where the undertakers will steward you across difficult slippery ground, like outriders; your boots will gather mud up the heels, but you will not stumble, you will carry her, you will carry her, all the way, you will carry her, steadily, so will your cousin, and the four other bearers, with an unrelieved ache, and

116

someone will have remembered roses to let go into the grave, and the gorse on the moorland, still flowering wildly, will smell almost like jasmine, and the rain will hold off, and the mountains will neither pity nor forgive you.

Live That You May Live

My daughter wakes in the night. Mummy, she calls, there's a bird! There's a bird in my bed!

I go into her room, switch on the bluish night light. She is standing up, holding the sheet above her head. Mummy, she says, the bird was flapping on my pillow. It was just a dream, I tell her. Lie down, go back to sleep. But Mummy, she says, its wing was on my face. Oh, that was just the blanket. No, Mummy, no. There's a bird. It was winding round my neck. It was trying to fly me.

Together we search behind the pillow. We look through her hair – tarnish-coloured, wild from its double crown – and under her small, bare feet. We unbutton her pyjamas, down the soft wall of her chest. Just a dream, I tell her. Lie down, go back to sleep. She sits and thinks for a moment. There's a dream and a bird in my bed, she says. She holds a finger to her lips. Shhh, Mummy, don't wake them. She settles on her side, feet splayed like a mermaid's tail, archer arms, her bow finger touching the wood's dark veneer. Childish. Mythic.

I kneel and stroke her back, tell her she is safe, tell her I am here. Her eyes are bright and open. My chased and searching girl. She is already quarry, already hunting reason, lost between imagined worlds.

So the artists make us. So the storytellers promise.

But I made her, in a womb once cut apart, stoned, and sewed. Cells and strings and hope. I made her bed – eight bolts, twelve screws, five panels of false mahogany – foolproof for skill-less artisans, unbreakable when she jumps. Nails, dovetails, glue. Mummy, she says, tell me a story, about birds and dreams and me. Hush, I say. Close your eyes, sleep. Tell me a story, Mummy, but only say what's true. The flicker of her old-gold lashes. A twitching foot. The rustling sheet. Then she is still and quiet. What shall I say?

Once there was a girl.

One night, when she was sleeping, birds came to take her. They were creatures of extraordinary plumage, white as fire, with beads of blood for eyes, and long necks that wound around each other. They came as if from nowhere, on creaking, muscled wings, calling out across the skies until they found her.

They lifted her bed upon their shoulders, bore it like a carriage from the house, and flew her up into the sky. They flew her far from home. All through the night her bed was towed. Up, over the little island and the great, cold roof of Europe. Over lands of men and commerce, where wars raged. Over lands of women, who wept and loved without hesitation. Over the smoke of poor villages and smouldering cities, valleys of wild red flowers, the longing sea.

They flew her along the withers of black mountains and down mirrored rivers, through great falling doorways of water, past empty palaces and earth-filled fountains, stone salons of fate and time. They flew her past the undecided moon.

She did not know where they would take her.

When they arced down, their wings beat sheets of cloud. Their beaks tore the shroud of night and let the sunlight enter. They came to ground on black webbed feet, the hot engines of their breasts cooling, landing the girl in places she could never have imagined. In raised and ropeless towers, shadowlands, broken reefs and windless deserts. In scented gardens and forcing houses, the lair of dragons, witches' caves. They set her gently into stiff schoolgirl shoes, green silk gowns and glass-edged heels, loaned from other women's wardrobes. They landed her into soldiers' boots, and baskets of fish carried by grandmothers. Into beauty, secrets and knowledge. Into the theatre of desire, where she saw the art of painted faces, lust's brokerage, holding fire inside the mouth and hand. Into the arms of unhearted men, and sick and ardent suitors, into the poet's hand, into love's abandoned chances.

They took her to the place where queens are made, from murderous ends, from iron tides, sacrifice, fury, tinder, powder, destructed elements, no materials known to man. The birds' feathers burned pale as fire. Her little bed was gone.

The birds left her there. They raised their wings, lifted their heavy bodies in the air, and, red-eyed, calling to each other, they flew on.

She called for her mother to come. She waited hours, days. She split her heart open and held it like two bowls to catch her tears. She drank the rain. She ate the snow. She watched the stars spin overhead, coveted as jewels, ruthless as choices. Then she lay down, curled warm inside her suffering. When she woke, she tried to find her way back home.

She walked. She ran. She rode the rumps of bony cows and breaching whales. She wove shoes from bark and wicker. She stole saucepans, coats and candles. She sold her hair to pay for bread. She followed the red throne of the setting sun.

On the way she slept in other beds. Beds left empty. Beds full of water. Beds made of timber, bone and silver. Beds carved from the forest's heart, hardwood that ballasted slaves, that glossed the emperor's table, built fortune's ports, drew coins slowly through its sap. Beds heavy as ice mantles, ordered for courtesans to serve the wealth of love's needs, cut by desire's machines. Beds

watched over by longing crowds and the creatures of the
sea. Beds in which she learned to read. In which she con-
ducted passion, rode lovers like falling trees, tasted rivers of seed, broke open others' hearts, was broken,
bound, was owned as she was free. Beds where she was
all her selves and none.

When she was alone again, she slept naked under
roofless stars, and in ocean rooms. In salted heavens,
libraries, frozen doorways, in grass forms on the moors.
She slept between the blue, spilled hearts of lakes, and
on the great, hot breasts of resting swans, inside the
belly of monsters, the very eye of the moon. She saw
light emptying and filling in the called-out skies. She
remembered flying. She looked for the birds, but they
were gone.

She walked. She ran. She joined the herds; she swam
with shoals. She caught eels and quartered them. She
drank wine and milk and milkless pauper's tea. She
learned to count money, learned to speak in tongues.
She painted mountains, mended torn hems and nets,
thatched, mapped waterways. She left suitcases on the
road. She forged papers. She crossed borders and crossed
borders and crossed borders, hoping to find where she
was going. She took the name of saints, hope, sorrow,
ruin, all her names, chosen, every one. She took titles,
husbands, brides, collected rings, memories of peat and silt
and hurt, carried lanterns, stone boats, blessings, coffins.

She burnt everything. Forgot the names of enemies. Forgot the name of her mother. She drew no face in the river. She believed only in living, believed in every breath, except the last. She did not find her home, though she had tirelessly travelled. She knew that she was made of roads; she knew moving was her spirit.

And so she lay in one last bed, unbreakable as death, and closed her eyes. And in her hand, plucked from the ashes, she held a feather.

Mummy, my daughter whispers. Tell me. But she is already sleeping. I draw the blanket up, turn out the light and close the door. She is another story, not this story. Not the archer, or the mermaid's foot, the queen or consul's wife, mistress, maker of peace or moons, mother of children, siren, widow, sign. She is not mine. She is of what I cannot know. Unmade. Ready. The birds are coming. They will wind her forward, every night. I will be old, and wakeful, my body too weak to build anything, mother to the daughter of time. They are coming on white, definite wings.

Acknowledgements and Thanks

Versions of these stories have been published or recorded by the following:

'Who Pays?' – *T* magazine (the *New York Times*), and *T24*, with Turkish translation by Aydin Mehmet Ali and Buğu M. Rıza

'Orton' – *The Amorist* magazine

'Sudden Traveller' – Audible Original's *Bard: The Short Story Collection*, the BBC and Comma Press

'Live That You May Live' (previously 'The Swan and the Courtesan') – Sotheby's

Thank you to Peter Hobbs, Kate Nintzel at Custom House and Lee Brackstone at Faber & Faber for editing work, to Silvia Crompton for copy-editing, and to Ellah Wakatama Allfrey, Damon Galgut, Andrew Miller, Jon McGregor, Rowan Pelling, Belinda Bamber, Tracy Bohan, Michael Miller, Lila Azam Zanganeh, Alex Bowler and Jane Kotapish for critical reading. The following people provided fantastic and generous assistance with research: Richard Thwaites, Jarred Mc-Ginnis, Metin Myumyun, Hamit and Necmettin Sert.

I am extremely grateful to the Royal Literary Fund for giving me a grant in 2017.

To those not already mentioned, who offered practical and creative support, love and kindness over the last few years – Anthony, Jonathan and Sally Hall, Fiona Renkin, Johanna Forster, Rebecca Watts, Eimear McBride, Naomi Wood, Imogen Cloet, Soyokaze Japanese, Norwich Montessori School, NR2 Supper Club and Blackbirds parents, Erik Rosenwood, Miss K. Stanley, Pete and Rowan again – THANK YOU.

To Hamit, teşekkür ederim, canım.

And Loy, my inspiring little traveller.

And Mum, you are in every page.